FLYAWAY

FLYAWAY

LYNN HALL

CHARLES SCRIBNER'S SONS
NEW YORK

F
HAL

Copyright © 1987 by Lynn Hall

Charles Scribner's Sons Books for Young Readers
Macmillan Publishing Company
866 Third Avenue, New York, NY 10022
Collier Macmillan Canada, Inc.

Printed in the United States of America
First Edition
10 9 8 7 6 5 4 3 2 1

Library of Congress Cataloging-in-Publication Data
Hall, Lynn.   Flyaway.
Summary: Ariel, a high school senior in Wisconsin, dreams of running away from her domineering father who selfishly controls her life and those of her mother and sister.
[1. Family problems—Fiction.   2. Fathers and daughters—Fiction.
3. Wisconsin—Fiction]   I. Title.
PZ7.H1458Fm   1987   [Fic]   87-12824
ISBN 0-684-18888-0

FLYAWAY

1

"Try them on here, where I can watch," he called. But I walked away.

They may have been bought with his money, these new wings of mine, but they were not his. I had earned them with a thousand humiliations, and they were not his.

I marched through the snow, my back stiffened against his voice at the back door. The binding clips on my boot toes made D-shaped prints in the new snow. A belt of trees separated our back yard from the golf course—black-etched oaks and pale aspen and dark green humps of cedar, with here and there a mammoth old pine looming like a mother. Sumacs and second-growth baby trees made a dense screen, head high, even in winter, so I didn't have to walk far to be invisible from the house.

This was my territory. The old snow beneath the new powder was corrugated with tracks from my outgrown skis; the sides of the pathway were dimpled with my pole marks. Just mine alone. No one else came here.

It was Christmas afternoon, the Christmas of my senior year. We were not allowed to come downstairs before eight o'clock on Christmas mornings, Robin and I, and when we did come down we were dressed for church. If I ever marry and have a family, we are all going to tumble down to the tree at dawn. We'll wear thick warm robes and huge woolly slippers with rabbit faces on the toes, even the adults. We'll plow into our presents before breakfast and throw the wrapping paper around. And we'll hug each other when we say thanks.

I have a whole collection of little dreams. Probably none of them will come true, but they keep me warm, playing them over for myself.

We came down to breakfast at eight, and Mother tied her apron over her church suit while she fried the eggs. My father wore a sprig of holly in his lapel, and a tie with a small red and green pattern in it. Joy to the world. He had laid a tiny holly corsage beside the plate of each of his three females, and we were to wear them to church, to show the town our family tradition.

"Robin, Ariel," he said to us as we sat down to breakfast, and like well-trained children we picked up our corsages and pinned them to our sweaters.

My father was not a tall man. He and I were eye-level that year, and Robin at fourteen was almost up to me. He was thick, though, through the middle. His shoulders were narrow and rounded, so that his overall shape was like a fence post, and his head was too small to match. He had thinning, colorless hair, and pale gray-green eyes behind his gold-rimmed glasses, and bits of gold showed in his mouth where false molars were wired to his real teeth. His skin was an oatmeal gray-tan color. I tried never to look at him, and touching him turned my stomach.

But fighting him was usually more trouble than it was worth, so Robin and I pinned on our badges of family unity and ate our Christmas breakfast—eggs and coffee cake, with grapefruit juice, which Robin and I forced down even though it tied our faces into grimaces and rippled sour shivers through our bodies.

I looked like Mother's daughter, a little taller than average, narrow and bony, sharp-featured and pale in coloring, with soft flyaway hair of a dull cream color. Robin was Father's daughter, everyone said. She was thicker-skinned and thicker-bodied, with pretty dark hair and eyes, from our father's father. She wore glasses, but they were as different in style from Father's as she could manage.

After the breakfast dishes were washed, dried, and put away, we sat in the living room and opened our gifts. Each of us had three. There were none from outside the family. Each of the gifts cost exactly twenty dollars, except those from Father. They were more expensive—the high points of the day, as they were intended to be. On the first of December each year, he gave Mother, Robin, and me sixty dollars to buy our three gifts, and he checked the price tags when we brought the gifts home, even on those bought for him.

How old was I, I wonder, before I'd realized that this was not the way money was handled in normal families?

My gifts from Mother and Robin were predictably nice. Within the twenty-dollar limit, we all hungered to *give*. From Mother, new blue knit ski gloves with white leather insets lining the fingers, and polypro linings. From Robin, a

3

book on cross-country ski techniques for advanced skiers, written by two Olympic team members.

And of course from Father, the new wings themselves. It was hard and terrible to love the gift while hating the giver, but through the years I had learned to make that separation. I blocked him out while I unwrapped the long narrow package, finding first the new poles, then the skis themselves.

The poles were longer than my old outgrown ones, pale blue with snowflakes, white wrist straps, and half-baskets at the tip.

The skis were so beautiful my breath caught; they stood taller than me, slim and light and graceful. They were Karhu Gazelles, candy-apple red with Karhu bears skiing on the tips. I turned the skis bottom to bottom and felt the stiffness of the camber, the curve in the middle that would lift me above the snow and let me glide on mirror-smooth tips and tails.

Setting them aside for Christmas morning church service and for the dinner afterward was torture. But finally, pantyhose, skirt, and sweater were gone, and I was in my own outer skin at last, my dark blue polypro ski underwear, windbreaker pants and jacket, my good old red cap and scarf, and the new blue gloves.

The sky was the same dirty gray as the ground. New snow fell in soft separate flakes that could be seen only against the black trees. The flakes kissed my face and melted there and I loved them. It was a warm afternoon, for central Wisconsin in December. There was no wind, just the tattered big snow-flakes and a sun that was merely a lemon shading in the gray sky.

I stood where my private trail emerged from the woods into a wide open valley spreading left and right. In summer this was the Heron Lake golf course, a green meadow doglegging between woods and the shore of our little lake. In winter it became part of a network of machine-molded cross-country ski trails maintained by three small guest lodges around the bend of the lake.

I looked left and right, and smiled. No one else in sight. Unusual for a Christmas afternoon in Heron Lake, but I was glad. I wanted my first flight on the new skis to be private. I'd been afraid of crowds of kids with new Christmas skis or of herds of holiday guests from the lodges. Or of Robin wanting to come along, since she inherited my old skis. But Robin was surprisingly tactful for her age; she knew when to leave me alone.

As I laid the gleaming red Gazelles in the track-machine's depressions, I felt a passing melancholy for the old skis that had been my love for the past three winters. They were too short for me now, and too soft in the camber arch, so that my increased weight flattened them in the middle, where the fish-scale pattern was carved to give grip on push-offs and uphill climbs. Flattened under too much weight, the old skis dragged.

"Okay, Gazelles," I said to them as I slipped my hands through the poles' loops and gripped. Ah, the handgrips felt good. It felt right, that three inches of extra length.

I fitted the metal D on the tip of my right boot into the ski's binding and pressed down. The clamp snapped and held. Ah. Good. Left foot snapped on, and I was ready. My heart thudded. Silly. They were only skis, only new skis.

I pushed off onto my right foot and tottered for an instant as the ski shot forward faster than I'd expected. With the next stride I was ready and balanced. The glide took my breath away. So fast. So smooth. Another push onto my right leg and I coasted yards down the trail.

My face flushed with excitement. I tucked and leaned into the speed, striding harder now, swinging my arms high, bringing them down into a leg-level pole plant that pushed me smoothly into the next stride. Like skating. Like running effortlessly.

Like skimming the ground on cardinal wings.

Up a long shallow incline where the old skis had plodded, the Gazelles carried me with their smooth glide only slightly shortened. They felt quick and poppy under my feet, spirited, like a thoroughbred horse or a fine sports car.

Level ground again. The clearing narrowed here, where belts of woods came close on both sides. The ice of the lake lay ahead and below, with dots of skaters on it. A skier appeared ahead of me, a tall humped male form.

"Track," I called gaily, although he was in another lane. He stepped aside and turned to smile. I lifted a pole to salute and skimmed past.

The ground sloped away in a short downhill run. A whoop escaped my throat as I crouched, balancing myself firmly with one ski slightly ahead. I stretched my arms forward, poles tucked neatly into my sides. I was perfect. My soul sang.

The Gazelles picked up speed at a rate that would have thrown me off if I hadn't been ready. The wind became ice against my face; the trees blurred as we passed. A curve approached. I carved into it with my outside ski, off-balanced for an instant, then caught myself and stood up slowly, relishing the long, long glide into a side trail.

Here a planting of young pine trees, only head high, sheltered families of wild turkeys. Their tracks and wing-trails were clear in the snow beside the ski trail. Cardinals decorated the pine branches and cursed me for my invasion.

"Joy to the world," I yelled at them, and they flew away, screeching at me.

"I'm going to do that, too, one of these days," I called after them. "I'm going to fly away."

2

I emerged from the woods trail onto the six-lane track leading past the warming hut. Here were the Christmas-afternoon crowds. Clots of slow beginners hampered my flight and sent me sidestepping from track to track, detouring them.

The warming hut was a sizable log building with a glass wall toward the south, for sun. In summer it was the golf-course pro shop; in winter it was operated by the three lodges as a convenience to skiers. I was thirsty from the sweat of my striding, so I dismounted and stood the Gazelles against the log rail with ranks of other skis, and went inside. I had no money to buy anything to drink, of course, but there was always water and hope.

It was too hot inside. Indoors always felt too hot after skiing. Along the back wall was a rustic refreshment bar, and along the window wall was a low bench. The man behind the bar knew me well enough to know I never bought anything, but since it was Christmas and he was feeling expan-

8

sive, he poured me a plastic cupful of hot spiced lemonade and gave it to me with a cinnamon stick stirrer and a Christmas napkin.

I thanked him and straddled the bench to look out at the white valley with its moving dots of skiers. The sun was almost out now; faint shadows leaned out from the upended skis.

"How is it out?" the barman asked. I figured he asked everyone the same thing, to make conversation, but I told him, "Perfect. Just a little dusting of new stuff, not enough to slow the tracks."

There were a dozen others in the room, milling around the displays of equipment or laughing among themselves. Some of the faces in the group were familiar, but I didn't feel I was one of them. I couldn't walk over and pull up a chair and laugh with them. I was Frank Brecht's daughter.

A couple came in, with a child between them. As the mother unwound her scarf, I saw that she was Mrs. Staas, my sixth-grade teacher. She bent to unwrap a boy of about seven or eight, while her husband ordered hot lemonades at the bar.

I remembered seeing that little boy around town. He was unusual looking, narrow-faced with a high bulging forehead and a mass of tight, mouse-colored curls. He looked middle-aged somehow, as though he were a musical prodigy or a tiny Einstein.

Mrs. Staas noticed me, grinned, asked if I was having a good Christmas, and accepted the hot cup from her husband with cold-stiffened fingers. I could see their redness from where I sat.

Her husband stood beside the bar, leaning on it with one elbow while he surveyed the room and the view beyond the window. To the barman he said, "We've got a new pair of Christmas skis here"—he nodded toward his son—"and I'm beginning to think we need some instruction. Who around here gives lessons, would you know?"

The barman, whose name was either Ben or Sam, I could never remember, said, "They've got an instructor over at Pinecrest if you'd want to try over there. I think they have beginner classes starting every couple of months."

"Do they have classes just for children, I wonder?"

Ben or Sam shook his head. "I don't think so. Just beginners, all ages."

I began to think.

I sat very quietly while the Staases finished their drinks and bundled up, then I followed them outside again and took a long time getting into my pole straps and ski bindings.

The three of them were trudging ahead of me on the first of the three beginner-trail loops, the little boy plopping his new skis awkwardly along, one parent on each side holding his elbows.

Poor little rat, he didn't have a chance of learning that way. I could hear the whine in his voice from where I skied along outside the track and several yards to the rear.

He fell, plopping his padded seat into the snow on his ski tails, and I could see by the stiffness in his back that he'd done it on purpose. He didn't want to be out here in the cold, doing something that was his parents' idea, not his.

I pushed off hard and glided up beside them as his parents levered him onto his feet by the elbows.

"Hi," I said directly to the boy. "Got new skis, I see. Those are good ones, too."

He looked up at me, scowling and hauling in on an obviously runny nose. To his mother, I smiled and said, "I

10

think you'd have better luck if you didn't hold onto his arms. You're throwing his balance off."

"We don't want him to fall and scare himself," the father said. But he spoke pleasantly.

"Oh, heck, falling's half the fun," I said, again talking directly into the scowling little face. "Look, it's not really falling, it's just making angels in the snow." And with upflung arms I fell sideways, then rolled over onto my back, waving the Gazelles over my head. The little guy grinned at me.

"Go ahead," I said to him. "Fall over and make a snow angel."

He pulled away from his parental training wheels and fell sideways like me, laughing when he found out it didn't hurt. I motioned his parents back and showed him how to roll up onto his knees, and stand up by himself.

We started off again, the little boy and I side by side in the tracks, his parents walking behind saying things like, "Careful, Jason, not too fast."

"Here, this is the way I learned," I said to him, and slipped the poles off his wrists. "You don't need poles to hold you up. Can you roller-skate?"

He nodded.

"Good. This is easier. Look, instead of walking on your skis, pretend they're skates. Just let your arms swing naturally. Don't worry about falling. You already found out that doesn't hurt. Okay now, push off on one foot and then the other one. Shift all your weight over to that forward foot. See? Look, like this."

He tried it and glided a yard before he over-balanced and fell. But when he got up, the narrow little face was knotted with concentration, and he pushed off again.

It was time.

11

I sidestepped close to Mrs. Staas and said, "I'm not a licensed instructor or anything, but I've been skiing for three years, I've got good books that I learned out of, and I can do anything except telemark turns. I'd be glad to give Jason lessons."

They looked at each other, and a married-couple message was telegraphed.

"How much would you charge?" Mr. Staas asked.

I knew that lessons at Pinecrest, in a beginners' class, cost ten dollars an hour. I had asked when I started skiing, knowing I had no money but just wanting to talk to someone about skiing.

"Ten dollars an hour," I said courageously. "I'm not as expert as a regular instructor, but on the other hand it would be private lessons."

They frowned a little at the expense. I said, "He probably wouldn't need more than six or eight, to get him started."

Small nods were exchanged between them and, grinning, we all agreed. For the next week, between Christmas and New Year's, they would bring Jason to the warming hut at two every afternoon.

"One thing," I said cautiously, "do you suppose you could, sort of, not tell anyone around town that I'm doing this? My dad's a little funny about us girls earning outside money. I guess he likes to provide us with everything. . . ." My voice became nervous-chattery before it petered out.

Mrs. Staas looked doubtful. "I don't know, Ariel, we don't want to be doing anything without your parents' permission." She was a teacher, after all. Parents' permission was the code teachers lived by.

I forced a confident smile. "Oh, that's no problem. I'll tell my mom I'm doing it. They know I'm out skiing every afternoon anyhow. It's not like I'd be someplace I wasn't supposed to be or doing something dangerous. We won't even get off the beginner trails."

We left it at that. The three of them reversed and plodded back toward the warming hut's parking lot, and I pushed off in a long glide full of escape and wild flapping excitement.

Sixty dollars. By the end of the week I would have sixty dollars that Father didn't know about. It would be the first money I had ever owned in my life.

I realized that was a bizarre statement for a seventeen-year-old girl living in the United States of America in the nineteen-eighties. But it was the truth. There had never been allowances, or baby-sitting earnings, or gift money from relatives. My father's family were all dead, and Mother's relatives had nothing to do with us. They used to give Robin and me birthday cards with money in them, until they found out that Father took the money and kept it—"for you. For your best interests."

In five short months I was going to be out of high school. Without money I would be a prisoner here in Heron Lake, where my father wanted me.

Without money for the escape.

Sixty dollars . . . not enough, but a tremendously exciting beginning.

Joy to the world! My Gazelles picked me up and carried me skimming, flying, toward a life that wasn't going to catch me and kill me after all.

13

3

After supper I asked permission to go to Marlee's, to see her presents and to tell her about my new skis. It was an ordinary request, and there was no problem about it. But of course I had to wait until Father's television show was over before he would drive me.

It was only four blocks to Marlee's house, and the streets of Heron Lake, Wisconsin, are totally safe, day or night, but that was the rule, and Robin and I had given up fighting it. If either of us went out after supper, Father drove us and picked us up. Period.

Most people around town thought Frank Brecht was a wonderful father. He was always at basketball games and PTA meetings, even committee meetings at our classmates' houses. He'd sit out in the car and wait for us. It embarrassed me and infuriated Robin, so gradually we quit being on committees. But to the rest of the town Frank Brecht was Father of the Century.

When his program was over he drove me the four blocks to Marlee's and left me, saying he'd be back in two hours. The car stayed purring in the driveway until I was in the house. One reason Marlee had evolved into my one and only friend was that she worked for my father in the drug store after school. Of course she didn't see him the way he was at home. No one did. But she saw enough of his fussy little habits at the store to believe what I told her about him. No one else would.

Marlee was very short, under five feet, and she was fat. She suffered agonies over it and ate hardly anything, but still she was fat. She had a very pretty face, beautiful pink-and-white skin, dark curly hair and brown eyes, and the most elegant eyebrows I'd ever seen. Like gull wings, and natural. Her face had the kind of turned-up features designed for smiling. And she always looked polished. She was neater and cleaner than anyone I'd ever known. I imagined that she was trying to make up for her poor oversized body. Sometimes I would look at her and realize that her cage was worse than mine.

She pulled me in through the front door and made me feel hugged without actually hugging me. She fluttered pats all over my arm and eased me out of my parka and steadied me while I toe-heeled out of my boots. She was wearing a new pink sweat suit with store tags still hanging from a side seam.

Marlee waved me through introductions to five or six visiting aunts and uncles who were crowded into the living room along with a huge Christmas tree, a real live tree, not like our metal Mountain King that Father assembled every year. This tree had a twisty trunk and drying needles, and it had to be steadied by twine tied to the stair bannister, but I loved it. It smelled like Christmas is supposed to smell.

15

Marlee's house was one of the big old Victorian ones built along the north corner of the lake by rich Chicago people as summer homes around the nineteen hundreds, when Heron Lake was in its glory. It sat across Shore Road from the lake, and up on a rise. It had wide, rounded porches on three sides, and a corner tower, and real wood wainscotting on the lower halves of the walls in the four big downstairs rooms.

I'd never seen the upstairs because it was closed off. The house had been in Marlee's mother's family for a long time. Two years earlier Marlee's father had wrenched his back taking a misstep backwards off a step stool while washing storm windows. He hadn't been able to work since then, so the family moved back to Heron Lake from Madison because they had inherited this house and thought they could live there cheaply. Marlee's mother worked as a checker at the Hy-Vee store, and her father built grandfather clocks from kits, which he tried to sell. There was not enough money to heat the huge old house, so they shut off the upstairs and lived downstairs.

We knelt beside the pile of packages under the tree while Marlee showed me her take: sweater, three pairs of earrings, cologne, a Wisconsin U sweat shirt, the usual. It made my three gifts seem slim until I thought about the Gazelles, and the afternoon's skiing, and Jason's lessons. Then, secure in my own wealth, I could admire her gifts, the tangible caring of aunts and uncles and parents.

We climbed across the welter of boxes and relatives and escaped to Marlee's room. It was a tiny box of a place behind the huge kitchen. Originally a maid's room, we thought.

Settling crosslegged on the bed, we got down to serious talking. I told her about the new Gazelles. She shook her head.

16

"That man."

"What?"

"Your father. He's a real artist at what he does. What did he give Robin?"

"A microscope. I don't follow you. What do you mean, an artist at what he does?"

"Playing this public role," she said patiently. "Can't you see the pattern, or are you too close to it? Your father loves this public image he's got, the image of the perfect husband and father. He drives your mom to the store every time she needs a loaf of bread."

"He has to," I snapped. "He won't let her drive, or have any money."

Marlee's hands rose and fluttered at me. "That's what I mean. He drives you over here and comes to fetch you. He buys you and Robin great Christmas presents so when you tell people about them, or when they see you out skiing, the whole town will think: Boy, that Frank Brecht is certainly a wonderful father."

I frowned and chewed my lip. "Do you think that's why he gives us such nice stuff, really? I always sort of thought it was just his way of showing he loved us—since he screws up every normal way."

I spoke lightly, but there was a small quaver underlining my words, and Marlee picked up on it. She was going to be an excellent social worker if she could ever scrape together the money for college, which was why she worked in the drug store.

"Well," she said placidly, "it doesn't really matter why he gives you stuff. With a man like that I guess you just have to take whatever you can get from him and not worry about the

17

rest of it. Other people have grown up without fatherly love and turned out all right. Just don't let it warp you."

I laughed at that. She was so obviously practicing for her social-worker career. Leaning closer, I said, "I haven't told you the best part. I'm going to be earning some money this week, and he doesn't know about it. Isn't that fantastic? When I was skiing this afternoon I ran into Mrs. Staas, she was my sixth-grade teacher, and she has this little boy, Jason. They got him skis for Christmas, but she and her husband didn't know beans about teaching him. They were holding him up by the elbows, for God's sake. So I offered to give him private lessons, ten dollars a lesson every afternoon this next week. Isn't that fantastic? If the weather stays decent, that will be fifty or sixty dollars."

Her eyes lighted up for me. "What will you do with it? Want me to keep it for you? I could hide it in my room."

"Would you? That would take care of that problem." There was no question about trust between us.

"What will you use it for?" she asked again.

My face glowed. I couldn't speak for a moment because the words were too big, too loaded.

"What, what?" she urged, bouncing on the bed.

"It's going to be my escape money."

"Sixty dollars? How far can you escape on that—Stevens Point? And what escape? When? Tell me."

We shifted closer until our knees were bumping and lowered our voices, even though we were alone at the back of the house.

"I don't know for sure how or where. All I know is I have to get out of that house. Mar, he's still saying I have to live at home after graduation and work in the drug store. For him.

18

Forever, unless a suitable husband comes along, and even then I'm not sure he wouldn't find some way to mess that up."

Marlee shook her head. "It's hard to believe, in this day and age. If I didn't know him a little bit myself, and if I didn't know what an honest person you are, I'd laugh off the whole idea. I mean, come on, no parent holds on like that any more. This isn't Victorian times. The whole thing is bizarre."

"The whole thing is sick," I said quietly. "He's made Mother into a shadow of himself. He makes prisoners of all three of us, and the sick part is that he doesn't love us. I know he doesn't. I think he hates us. I think he hates all women, and for some twisted reason he has to keep Mother and Robin and me under his thumb to kind of, I don't know, punish us or something. Punish us for being female, maybe. I don't know."

We sat silently. Marlee's hands and wrists were tiny compared with the rest of her, tiny and soft and expressive. Of their own accord, they patted my arms and knees while she said, "Listen, Ariel, you just hang on to what I keep telling you. Don't let him damage you. Hold on to your own strength until you can get away from him. Sixty dollars might not get you very far, but you've got me pulling for you. God, I wish I had money to contribute to the cause. The Ariel Freedom Fund."

"I know. I know you'd help if you could. But your escape is just as important. You've got your heart set on a career that needs college degrees, and I know that's where every penny you can scrape up has to go. At least my goal isn't that expen-

19

sive, just enough money to get me to a town big enough to hide in. Enough to survive on till I can get any kind of job. I might even be able to do it on the Jason money if I work it right."

Her hands gripped mine then, and our eyes locked, fusing our wills.

4

My father drove into Marlee's driveway promptly at ten. I was watching from the living room window with my parka on, because he didn't like delays.

Marlee's mother, as she patted me toward the door, said, "You don't know how lucky you are to have a father like that, going to so much trouble so you and Robin never have to walk anywhere on these cold nights."

She was a good-hearted woman, the picture of Marlee thirty years older, and I knew she meant it as a compliment, so I didn't answer honestly.

"I know it," I said, "G'night, merry Christmas. Marlee, I'll stop by tomorrow afternoon, about that . . ."

She nodded, we waved, I ran.

He leaned across the car seat to push open the door. Around his neck was the tan wool scarf I'd bought for him with his money and wrapped and tagged and laid under the tree. It had cost exactly twenty dollars, with tax and wrapping

21

paper and bow. He'd known what was in the package because he'd checked the store receipts. Still, he'd looked pleased when he opened the box, and now he was ostentatiously wearing the scarf.

A very old ache flashed through me, a hunger for a genuine father, even an out-of-work one like Marlee's.

"Did you have a good visit?"

I nodded.

"What did you talk about?"

Silently, I flared at him. Oh, come on, Father, can't I have even that much privacy? Grimly, I lied to him. "Marlee has a new boyfriend. At least she likes him, but that's as far as it's gone yet."

"She'd better beware," he said through tightened lips. "A girl with her appearance, no decent boy is going to be taking up with her. She'd be better off to concentrate on her career and forget about boys."

I didn't try to defend her. He heard only what he wanted to hear. The car turned away from our street and into the main business street, two blocks of low store buildings facing the west shore of the lake. A strip of park separated water from street. The open-walled shelter house held stacks of picnic tables covered with snow.

We parked in front of the drug store while Father bounced across the sidewalk to check the locks on the front door. It was a narrow corner drug store, left over from an earlier generation. Two steps led up to the inset corner door, and display windows held pyramids of cologne and bath powder.

The town assumed that my father owned the drug store. Probably a few men from the bank or adjoining businesses knew that he only managed it, that Frank Brecht was no more than a pharmacist working for a man in Milwaukee who owned the property. No one in our family ever said anything around town to correct that misconception.

When the store's security was assured we drove on toward home. Thinking along the lines of what he'd been saying about Marlee, I said, "Father, I'm a senior this year, you know."

He shot me a look to see if I was being sarcastic. Sarcasm wasn't allowed. "I'm well aware of that, Ariel."

"Are you also aware that in a few months there will be things like my senior prom? If I get a date for it, are you going to let me go, or are you going to drive me there yourself, or what?"

He started to answer, caught himself, and pondered. I could almost read the thoughts flashing behind his eyes. No date for the senior prom would mean that Ariel Brecht was in some way a failure. Other, less attractive girls would have dates. Other fathers would be seen allowing some freedom at graduation time, even very strict fathers. If Frank Brecht didn't unbend a little, it might be talked about around town. Hanging on too tightly, they might say. Or, poor Ariel couldn't get a date, they might say. Not pretty enough?

Carefully, Father said, "As long as I approved of the boy and his family, certainly you could go out under those circumstances. With curfew, of course."

I kept my sigh silent and proceeded with the negotiations. An idea was beginning to surface. If I had the Jason money and an accepted boyfriend who might be willing to help, the escape might not be impossible. . . .

"You know," I said smoothly, "a girl doesn't just get a prom date. Not in a school this small. It's usually somebody she's been going with through the year. If I had to wait till the last minute and just hope somebody would know that I was available, I'd be stuck with the worst guy in the class. As things are now, nobody ever asks me out because they figure you're not letting me date yet."

I screened the hatred out of my voice and held it level. He said nothing. We were almost home. I pressed on.

"So, what I mean is, if somebody were to come along between now and graduation and ask me for a date, it might be a good idea to go out a few times. . . ."

He looked at me keenly as he switched off the ignition. "Are you being honest with me, Ariel? Have you started something with some boy I don't know about?"

"No. I haven't. I'm just looking ahead to possibilities. I'm just saying *what if?*"

He cleared his throat and got out of the car. Like a well-trained young lady, I sat still until he opened my door and handed me out. Walking toward the house, he said, "If that occasion arises, we'll see."

It was better than I'd hoped for. Now all I had to do was find a boyfriend in the next few months, one honest enough to pass Father's inspection and dishonest enough to help me when I made my getaway.

5

Our house, like Marlee's, had been built eighty years earlier as a vacation home. Originally it had sat in the middle of several acres of rolling, tree-dotted lawn that went all the way back to the lake. Now most of the lawn was eaten up by Pine Street and a row of newer houses to the front and sides, the golf course to the rear. Whatever grandeur the house might have started with had melted away now into the neighborhood.

The house was built of local fieldstone, small rounded rocks in shades of pink and blue and gray. It wasn't a big house like Marlee's, but it was maintained much better. The trim and doors got a fresh coat of dark red paint every third year. The house had steep roof pitches and dormers jutting out on both sides, and small round windows at the gable ends.

I noticed things like that about houses, and I'd done quite a bit of sketching of the houses around town that I liked best.

There were dreams and futures waiting for me beyond this year, and I could feel myself expanding toward them when I drew houses. Architect? Interior designer? Landscape designer? It was all possible, if only . . .

I hung my parka in the front closet, recited to Father, "Thank you for picking me up," and went upstairs. The upper story was smaller than downstairs, just two slant-roofed bedrooms tucked in under the eaves. Our parents' room was downstairs, built on to the back of the house. That should have given Robin and me a nice lot of privacy, but we never knew when Father was going to look in on us.

There was no light under Robin's door, but I could hear her radio, so I went in. It was only a little after ten. I turned on the light, and she grimaced and threw her arm over her eyes.

"I thought you'd still be hard at it with the microscope," I said. Robin's room looked like a junior high science fair. It was cluttered with butterfly boards, jars of moth cocoons, waxed leaf collections and heaps of *Ranger Rick* and *Natural Science* magazines. The new microscope was still in its red-and-yellow box.

She sat up, turned down the radio, and hunched in a wrinkled pile in the bed. I shifted a mound of dirty clothes from the corner of the bed and sat.

"Haven't you even tried it out yet?" I asked, nodding toward the microscope. It was a student's model, with packets of slide glasses and samples of things to look at. It was just right for Robin, as my Gazelles were just right for me.

She shook her head. "Nah, I'll try it tomorrow maybe."

"You're being stupid, Rob. It's a great microscope. You should be enjoying it."

"It costs too much," she said fiercely.

26

I shrugged. "So would my skis, if I let myself think about it that way. I don't like having to be grateful to him any more than you do."

"Then how can you take what he gives us and enjoy it? God, Arie, I look at that scope and I'm dying to get my hands on it, but every time I do I think, if I enjoy something Dad gave me, I'm giving in to him. You know? It's like he's buying me. Like my price is a microscope, and your price is a good pair of skis, and that's all he has to do, to get us."

"He hasn't got me, or you, but it's stupid not to enjoy the thing, the scope or the skis or whatever. Look at it this way. All that birthday money we used to get from Gramma and Grampa Burnett? I just figure that's the money that bought my skis."

She knotted her face and considered. Without her glasses Robin looked unfocused and vulnerable. Small red spots astride the bridge of her nose showed where the glasses sat. One of the spots was blistered.

"You need to get your glasses adjusted again," I said.

"What all did Marlee get?"

I recited the list: sweat suit, jewelry, sweater. Then I told her about the Jason lessons and the money that was going to be mine—hidden at Marlee's house but mine to use for my escape.

"And something else," I said when that had been discussed and gloated over. "Just now I asked him if he'd let me go out on a few dates if I got asked, just so I'd have a date for the prom, you know. And he said possibly, if he approved of the guy and if we kept the curfew and all that stuff. So! If I can just find somebody—it doesn't have to be any big romance or anything like that—just somebody with a car, to help me get away."

27

Robin and I had always talked about our escapes. They were the springboard for all our daydreams. We both understood from an early age that we could not survive intact in this household.

We talked on until Father came upstairs to separate us with his good night. In my own bed across the hall, I lay thinking about the next few months, about how to engineer my escape. About Robin, who would be following me a few years from now.

I didn't worry so much about her. In spite of the fact that she was able to call him Dad while I could not unbend beyond Father, her hatred was hotter and stronger than mine, and nearer the surface. When the time came, she would explode out of that house propelled by her own rocket power.

For me it was going to be harder, because I was weakened by caring about Mother, and even, in some perverse way, caring about him. Not love, not the kind of love every daughter should feel for her father, but a black-hole kind of aching, I don't know, a hunger for something that wasn't quite there.

I truly wanted those skis to have been his way of showing affection.

Robin was probably wiser than me, or stronger. Her microscope was still in its box. She would escape intact.

For me, there was the danger that my softening needs might keep me in this house, in the life he dictated for me, until it was too late to escape. Until my will was eroded by convenience.

Mrs. Staas gave me the ten-dollar bill even before the lesson began. I slipped the bill inside my ski glove so I could feel the papery warmth of it rubbing against my palm. The first money I ever owned. The consciousness of it warmed my hand, my arm.

It was the key to everything. With money I could pay for a glass of hot lemonade at the warming-hut bar and not have to wait for the pity or generosity of others. With this ten dollars I could buy a pair of ski bones to hold my Gazelles together so they wouldn't slither awkwardly in my fingers when I carried them. With enough ten dollarses I could buy anything I wanted.

And I would. With this seed money, hoarded at Marlee's and not wasted on small wants, I would buy my way into another life, and in that life would be jobs, paychecks, a normal existence.

"Have a good time, now," Mrs. Staas said. "I'll meet you here in an hour."

Jason looked smaller than I remembered him, just a pair of huge dark eyes looking dubiously out from between scarf and cap. He was bundled up rigidly. Far too many clothes for cross-country. I forgot the bill in my palm and beamed all my attention at Jason.

We walked to a deserted stretch of beginner trail, and I showed him how to slip his hands through the pole loops. "Like this, loop up, reach through, then drop so the loop comes across your palm. That way you can bear down on the loop when you push off, and hinge the pole out behind you. Don't worry about all that now, you'll see the logic when we get started."

The afternoon was warm and sunny, pleasant for earlobes but not good for the snow, which was melty and grabby against my skis. I couldn't have flown anyway, with Jason in tow, so I unzipped both of our jackets and enjoyed the warmth.

At first Jason took carefully planted steps, leaning on each pole as he went, but with a little fooling and falling on my part, he began to relax.

"That's it," I cheered. "Push off onto this leg as soon as your weight has come forward above this leg. Push off hard now, just like skating. Forget about your poles. Just let your arms swing naturally. There you go. Ooops."

We laughed as he overbalanced and sprawled in the snow.

By the end of the hour he was unwrapped, unscarfed, rosy-faced and sweating lightly. And he didn't want to go back to the car.

"I want to go down a hill," he demanded.

"Maybe tomorrow, a small hill. But first you have to learn

30

to walk up it. You have to pay the price of walking up before you can have the fun of sliding down."

"He did great," I told Mrs. Staas when I delivered him back to the parking lot.

"I did great, Mom. I went as fast as Ariel, and she fell down more than me. Tomorrow she's going to teach me to do hills. But I have to climb up them before I can go down."

"Just a teeny little hill," I said in response to Mrs. Staas's worried expression.

When they had driven away I parked my Gazelles beside the warming hut and went inside. I'd been out on the trails for two hours before Jason's lesson, trying to master Wipeout Hill, and I was ready for some sitting and a drink of something, anything.

The room was full of milling, laughing, sweating skiers. A beautiful afternoon, Christmas holiday in Heron Lake, what else did I expect? This town was not a big resort area, not like Telemark and Eagle River and Spring Green. It didn't draw piles of tourists from the cities, but the local people were outdoor-oriented. That was probably why they chose to live here. But they weren't the rich outdoor-sports types. Fishing was bigger in summer than waterskiing. Deer hunting, and squirrel and pheasant, and trapping: those were the fall excitements. Snowmobiling and cross-country, ice skating on the lake: that was winter at Heron Lake. There were a few small downhill-ski areas, but not many of the local people bothered with that.

So most of the faces above new Christmas sweaters and tight nylon bib-suits were familiar. I tucked my money into the zip pocket of my windbreaker pants, hung my jacket on top of three others on a peg near the door, and made my way through the bodies toward the window bench, sniffing the inevitable cold nose drips and pushing up my sweater sleeves.

With Father's tentative permission in mind, I scanned the room for potential boyfriends while trying to look casual. Just casually glance around, see who's here, I told myself. Don't make eye contact with anyone.

There were half-a-dozen kids from school, but they all seemed to be there in pairs. I hated that. I felt glaringly alone, obviously unchosen.

And without a drink in my hand I felt awkward, as though I had no right to be sitting in the warming hut at all. Sam or Ben, the bar guy, was too busy with paying customers to notice my empty right hand. I looked around and spotted, on the low window ledge behind the bench where I sat, a Styrofoam cup with an inch of something brown left in it. On the rim was a clear cracked bright pink pattern of a lipstick mouth.

I picked up the cup, hid the lipstick mark with my hand, and drank a sip. It was terrible, coffee gone stone cold. But it was a cup to hold, anyway. As long as no one saw me actually picking it up. . . .

Casually, I glanced around the room again and met a pair of eyes. Mocking.

His name was Jens something. He'd graduated the year before. Even in a high school as small as Heron Lake, two people as inconspicuous as this Jens guy and me could coexist without ever crossing paths. I wasn't even entirely sure of his name.

He was extremely tall and thin, with pale colorless hair cut so short it hardly showed up on his skull. He wasn't good looking, but in my state of need, that was a plus. The good-looking guys were always spoken for, and they wouldn't have been interested in me.

This Jens didn't appear to be with anyone. He'd been lounging against the bar, in loose conversation with two older men but looking around the room, essentially unconnected. He would have been a possibility if only he hadn't seen me pick up a stray cup and drink from it. My face burned and I looked away from him. He pushed off from the bar; I saw the motion from the corner of my eye. He might or might not have been headed toward me, but I couldn't take that chance. I dismounted my straddle position on the bench, flagrantly deposited the cup in the trash barrel, and escaped, zipping my jacket outdoors.

I skied home by the most direct trail, going against the flow of traffic as most of the afternoon's skiers began moving toward the hut and their cars. The afternoon was chilling now that the sun was lower and weaker, just above the rim of pines.

Pausing in the house only long enough to rack my skies on the back porch and change from ski boots into regular boots, I walked the few blocks downtown. Paranoid I may have been, but I did not want my ten-dollar bill under my father's roof for even a few hours.

If I were to walk into that drug store eighty years from now, blindfolded, the smell of it would take me back to my childhood. I couldn't begin to analyze the ingredients in the bouquet, but they were underscored by musty old building and overlaid with bath powder.

The main room was long and narrow and dark, the waffled tin ceiling too high for good lighting. Tall shelves divided the space; children could pocket small cologne bottles and get away without being seen. At the far end of the room, raised by one step and hedged by a glass partition, was my father's kingdom, the pharmacy counter. He seldom emerged; as the pharmacist, he was above waiting on customers. The Dr. Scholls footpads and the disposable nursing bottles and the earwax dissolvers were Marlee's responsibility.

She was the heart of the store, her round pink face glowing with warmth for whoever came within range. She wore a pale blue store smock. Idly, I turned the paperback book carrousel while Marlee waited on three old ladies. Then I moved toward the front of the store, where dental floss and false-teeth glue blocked Father's view.

She came up close beside me, and my hand, with the ten-dollar bill folded damply within it, dove into Marlee's smock pocket and left the nest egg there.

7

Mother and I had lunch alone the next day. Robin had recently begun an intense friendship with Amy Stendorf, who lived three doors down from us, across the street. Amy was two years younger than Robin, and the difference between twelve and fourteen is much more than two years, so the friendship surprised me. It pleased Father, though, and he allowed Robin to eat lunch sometimes at Amy's house, as long as Robin called him first, at the store, and asked permission. I believe he felt that Amy would have a slowing effect on Robin's maturity.

I stiffened during lone lunches with Mother. We had nothing to talk about. I dared not tell her about the Jason lessons. I didn't believe she would risk keeping a secret from Father. And so we ate with our attention on our plates, and I left as soon as possible.

In our house, no one helped Mother with meals or dishes. The housework in all its aspects was Mother's justification for existence. Father earned the money and handled it. Mother took care of our bodily needs and the house. Robin and I were students. Everything categorized, with no relation to the real world at all. It was as though Father had plucked our lives from a Victorian novel.

So I left her carrying dishes to the sink and escaped on my lean red Gazelles into the forest. It was colder now. The snow was crusted with pebbly ice, from yesterday's melt, so my skis alternately skidded gripless in the tracks or broke through the crust to drag, crunching, against its edges. It was no day to teach Jason downhill technique.

I waited for him in the warming hut, hoping for someone interesting to come in, but there were few skiers.

By the time Jason arrived, the track-grooming machine had been over the beginner trails, breaking the ice crust and mixing it with the softer snow beneath. The mix felt good against the grip section of my skis, just under my feet.

We found a small hill and I showed him how to walk up without leaning forward, how to herringbone and sidestep for hills too steep to walk up. Then, on the gentle downhill side, we coasted and he fell and we laughed and tried again.

"Bend your knees a little more," I told him. "Stay loose. Relax every muscle except what you absolutely need to stand up. That's good. Hands out front, tuck your poles up under your elbows, there you go. You look terrific. Push off easy now. Keep your weight leaning forward into the hill."

He had a small child's natural looseness and balance, and after the third try he was looking for bigger hills.

At the end of the hour I handed a glowing, chattering boy back to his mother in exchange for two five-dollar bills. After a quick breather in the warming hut, I went out again and circled the main valley on an intermediate trail that led to a steep wooded slope above the lake.

Wipeout Hill was my own private name for that stretch of trail. There were other, steeper hills on the trails designated expert-level, and I'd managed most of them reasonably well, at least on my old, slower skis. But this intermediate-level hill was for some reason my Waterloo.

It began steeply, with a quick dogleg to the left, leveled slightly, then curved sharply to the right, where a series of roller-coaster bumps waited to throw anyone who was still slightly off-balance from the sharp right turn. On downhill skis these turns would have been simple, but the narrow cross-country skis lacked the edging for swift turn-control: body balance was crucial, and digging the ski edge into the snow to carve a turn was much harder.

I poised at the crest of the hill, focusing on the tracks in front of me rather than on the trees crowding in too close at the edges. In my mind I rehearsed each shift of body weight necessary to get me through the dogleg and around that right turn. I shook the tension out of my hands, flexed my knees deeply, moved my right ski forward a foot, ready for the first left turn into the dogleg.

With a tremor of fear-laced excitement, I pushed off. I bore down on my right ski, edging hard just before the dogleg turn, then switched quickly for the right turn. The Gazelles took me faster than I'd ever flown this hill. Coming out of the second dogleg corner I overbalanced and fell, sliding several yards on the icy snow before I rolled to a stop.

Grimly I trudged back up to the starting place, analyzing the error. Again I pushed off, more cautiously this time, so that my speed wasn't so great. Both dogleg turns whipped past under the Gazelles and I was still upright. I bent deeper, left ski forward, fists straight ahead on an imaginary steering wheel.

The sharp right turn, rimmed with trees, came at me. Beyond the turn a figure came into sight, trudging up the hill.

"Track," I yelled.

The turn was on me. Left ski out of the track and pigeon-toed into a half-snowplow, right shoulder back, weight over the outside ski. I bore down hard on the edged left ski and felt it push me perfectly into the turn while the deep rut of the track carried the off-weighted right ski around the bend.

The crash was unexpected, body impact with something dark and giving. Not a tree; I knew that as I somersaulted down the hill, skis and poles angling through the air like pick-up-sticks.

My legs and skis were so tangled I had to release one toe-clamp and kick free of the ski before I could roll up onto my knees. Snow was inside my cuffs, and my right thumb hurt. The pole loop must have bent it backward as I somersaulted. There was snow down the back of my neck, too, I realized as I stood up and stamped back onto my ski.

Another figure farther up the hill was climbing to its feet, too. As we approached each other I recognized the Jens guy from the embarrassing coffee cup incident the day before.

I pulled off my cap to whap the snow from it. "I yelled track. Why didn't you get out of my way?" I snapped at him.

He grinned.

"What are you smiling at?" Was he an idiot?

"Your hair is standing straight up," he said.

I have very fine thin hair, and static electricity does make it fly away or cling to my forehead, or both. Quickly I pulled my wool cap back on.

"Why didn't you get out of my way?" I snapped again. I wasn't thinking of him as boyfriend potential, only as a trail-rude idiot skier who had messed up my best run yet and endangered both our necks.

"Why didn't you get out of mine?" he countered blandly.

"I was in the right-hand lane."

"That doesn't have anything to do with it, stupid. The downhill skier always has the right of way over the uphill one because they don't have as much control. Oh, well." I began to simmer down and remember that he was a boyfriend possibility and I was desperate.

Seeing him up close, I could tell his hairline had already begun to recede at the corners of his long Scandinavian face. His mouth was crowded with long dingy teeth, and his eyes were small and pale. But I could live with imperfections like that for the few months it would take to finish school and get away. I smiled my best, warmest smile.

"Well, just so we both survived."

I was prepared to go along in his direction, but he reversed and came with me down the rest of the hill, over the roller-coaster bumps and around a gentler right turn where the trail leveled and followed the lake shore. He drew up beside me in the multi-lane track, and we moved in a rhythmic arm-swinging glide-stride. The arc of his poles forced my poles in close to my skis, but since his carriage was stiff and upright I assumed he was a beginner and probably didn't realize he was hogging the space.

We talked: I knew you at school, didn't I? What year are you? What are you doing now? The standard mutual ground.

39

He had graduated the year before and was temporarily working with his dad, while trying to get into college. He was going to be a basketball coach, he told me, but hadn't been able to get into the University of Wisconsin that year.

"I thought I could get in on an athletic scholarship," he said, a little breathless by now from keeping up with me. "So when that fell through I didn't have tuition money, so I thought, heck, I'll stay home a year and work for my dad, stash a little cash, and go next year."

When we got back to the warming hut he asked me in for a hot drink. He didn't mention the coffee-cup incident, and of course I didn't either. We sat together on the window bench between piles of other people's jackets, and I was able to look Sam or Ben in the eye, as a genuine cash customer.

"I'll run you home," he said after an hour of talk.

I shook my head. "Thanks, but my father is really strict about things like that." In a town this size, there was too much danger of someone seeing an unauthorized ride and mentioning it to Father.

"Does he let you go out?" Jens asked.

I cheered silently. "Yes, but only if he approves of you first."

Jens smiled, and I was startled to see a gleam of proprietary pride on his face. Was he gloating at having discovered a fair maiden whose purity was protected by a dragon?

"Your father owns the drug store, doesn't he?" Jens asked. "I'll stop in there and butter him up a little. Tomorrow night okay?"

I nodded, careful to control the elation swelling in my chest. A cash-paying secret job and a boyfriend-ally all in one week. It was probably too good to last, but I intended to enjoy it to the hilt while it did.

40

8

Robin and I never invited friends to our house for supper. Marlee had come once but never came again, and I was relieved. The supper misery always began with the milk.

Robin and I each drank a glass of milk with our supper. An ordinary, even caring paternal rule, it might seem to an outsider. But for Robin it was an ongoing humiliation. Years ago, when we were both small, Father had insisted on our drinking milk that had soured slightly in the refrigerator. We told him it didn't taste good, but he made us drink it anyway.

Although I never liked milk after that, I did learn to force down my distaste and my glass of milk every night. For Robin it was worse. Milk triggered a gag reaction in her. She wept and spat up at the table and finally was made to stand at the kitchen sink, alternately drinking, crying, and gagging, every night of her life, until a full glass of milk had been consumed.

He stood in the kitchen with her, to see that she didn't

pour it down the drain. They said nothing to each other until they were back in the dining room, seated. But her hate was palpable.

The other reason we didn't want our friends to see our suppers was that Mother rarely sat at the table. She brought dishes in and passed them, carried them back to the kitchen, and ate her meal in bites between serving and packing the leftovers into plastic refrigerator boxes.

When I was first old enough to see that this wasn't right, I complained. "No," she said, "I'd rather do it this way. I'm never hungry at night anyway, and this way I don't have a pile of dishes to do afterwards."

Hot water filled the sink as soon as Robin's milk drinking was out of the way, and every dish that came from the dining room went directly into the suds. It might have been an efficient system, it might possibly have been her preference, but it set my teeth on edge even after all those years.

That night when Robin and Father came back from the kitchen and settled at the table with me, he said, "Apparently you've been doing more than skiing these afternoons, Ariel."

I thought of the Jason lessons, and tensed. In my mind I began preparing a statement. I'd been helping a little kid learn to ski. His parents didn't know anything about it . . . no mention of money.

He went on. "Jens Jensen stopped in the store this afternoon. He said he'd met you skiing and wanted to take you out to dinner tomorrow night. He asked quite politely."

I held my breath.

He raised his voice toward the kitchen and said, "Judith, Mrs. Kritz was in again today, comparing prices. She hasn't bought her medication from me in three months, and I know she's still on it. She has to be. These senior-citizen maga-

42

zines are actually promoting generic drugs now. Actually advertising them and encouraging people to order generic drugs at cut rates. Something needs to be done about this trend."

"Father," I said, with a tinny note in my voice, "what about Jens? Is it all right?"

He leveled his glasses at me, and his thin lips disappeared into a tight crack. "I told him it would be all right this once, on a trial basis. I know the family. They're not on our level, but they seem honest enough. He's to pick you up at six, you're going to the Antlers, and you'll be home by nine."

I didn't know whether to cheer or cringe. It was hard to imagine any nineteen-year-old allowing his date's father to set rules like that. This would very probably be a one-time date. Still, it was a date.

Father cleared his throat and said, "Robin, I want you to take Ariel's old skis and begin learning on them. Ariel, you'll take your sister with you whenever you ski."

Robin opened her mouth to wail, and we looked at each other with silent dismay. There was no need to ask the reason for this new rule. I had picked up a boy on the ski trails, an apparently acceptable one this time, but that bit of freedom frightened him. Neither of us argued the edict. We would find our own circumventions.

After supper I asked Father's permission to make a phone call, and invited Marlee over. I'd have preferred to go to her house, but this was Father's board meeting night at the church, and he'd be tied up too late to pick me up.

We settled on my bed, Robin, Marlee and I, and Marlee tucked away my five-dollar bills in her purse.

I told her about Jens, and our date.

Robin said, "Yeah, and now I have to go skiing every time Arie wants to, just so she won't be picking up boys. I don't know why he thinks I'd tattle anything to him. I mean, you'd think he'd know Arie and I are on the same side, against him."

"Don't worry about it," I told her. "I'll show you how to get around on the skis a little bit, and you can just cut around the end of the street and get over to Amy's along the edge of that hay field."

"Or I'll pick up guys myself," she muttered. "Maybe with any luck I'll get pregnant and he'll disown me. Or kill me, whichever."

Marlee stretched out across the head of the bed. "Does he ever hit you guys or do anything physical like that?" she asked in her social-worker voice.

I shook my head. "I don't think he ever had to. We were just always so intimidated by him, all he ever had to do was give us that look." And I pulled my face into Father's scowl. We giggled, then glanced toward the door. He was at his board meeting and Mother's television was on in the living room, so we were probably safe, laughing.

Marlee said, "I can't get over him letting you have a date."

"I can't get over any guy putting up with all that grilling, just to go out with me."

"Marry him," Robin said abruptly.

"What?"

"Marry this Jens guy. That'd be an easier way out of this place than trying to run away to some city and getting a job."

I rolled over on my back and hugged a pillow. "I couldn't marry him. He's got this huge mouthful of crooked teeth. And he's starting to get bald already at the age of nineteen. I'd end up with six bald buck-teethed children. Jens Junior and Lars and Olie . . ."

A pillow smothered my face.

44

"Seriously though," Marlee said when she and Robin had stopped tickling and smothering me, "maybe you should think about marriage as a possible way out. Robin's got a point. Once you're eighteen and legally married, he couldn't do a thing to you."

"Yeah, but that's no reason to get married. Come on. Marry some guy I don't even love, just to get away from my father? I could be getting into something even worse."

The three of us looked at each other, telegraphing the same thought. There was nothing worse.

Marlee said, "Look what he's done to your mom. He's had her under his thumb so long she's not even her own person anymore. If you asked her what she thought about the weather she'd have to check to see what Frank's opinion was. If she had any willpower left at all, she'd never let him get away with this tyranny. I'm sure she didn't start out being that spineless."

"She was pretty young when they got married," Robin said. "Seventeen, I think."

"That makes a difference," Marlee said soberly. "Not too many seventeen-year-olds have much self-confidence. I can say that for sure because I am one. You know what I mean, Arie. Look at the kids we know at school, even the ones that seem like they've got it all together. You know darn well there's a scared little kid hiding inside just about everybody in our class, if we just knew them well enough to see it. Somebody at that stage of her life marries some guy that she looks up to and believes everything he says, and pretty soon he starts squelching her, telling her she's stupid or ugly or whatever. She's going to believe him. A guy with as much hate and disrespect for women as your dad . . . just think of the damage he could do to a young wife's self-esteem."

45

"Well that's true," I said, "but part of it is her fault, too. I mean, there are no tyrants without victims, and I doubt she ever really fought him when they started out together. If she hadn't stood for that kind of treatment, probably none of us would have to live with it now. I blame her, too."

Marlee sat up to pontificate. "The main thing, like I keep telling you, is not to let your messed-up parents screw up your life for you. You just about have to stay here till you get out of high school anyway, because you can't go anywhere without that diploma. But if either one of you stays one minute more than you have to, you're crazy."

"Well, I'm not about to take four more years of this," Robin muttered. She rolled off the bed and went to the window to lean her forehead against the cold glass. "I'm not sure yet how I'm going to do it, but one of these days . . ."

Marlee and I glanced at each other, then at Robin's back. The intensity in my sister's voice was chilling.

"Don't do anything crazy, Rob," I said. "You're only fourteen. You couldn't begin to support yourself for at least a couple of more years. You don't want to end up in a prostitution ring somewhere."

"Why not?" she asked bleakly.

After a long pause I said, "Because I need you here, for one thing. You stick it out until I get away and get set up someplace, and then you can come live with me."

"I don't know if I can last that long," she said. "I honestly don't."

9

The Antlers was an old hotel on Main Street, across the street from the drug store. Only a few old people lived in the hotel now, but the restaurant on the main floor was one of the better places in town to eat. Most Sundays our family ate dinner there after church. I think Father was parading his family, his family-ness, in front of the town. Quite a few families from church ate there, placid with tradition and the morning services.

It felt different now, walking into the dining room in front of Jens. He had hung our jackets on the coatrack in the entryway, and with his fingertips at the small of my back, steered me toward an empty table. I had the queer sensation of having exchanged Father for this tall, sweaty-handed young man.

The room was too garishly lighted, and the surfaces were too harsh. Linoleum floors and yellow plastic tabletops of-

47

fended my vision of elegant date-dining. On each square table stood a bud vase with yellow and orange plastic roses.

In my next life, as a secretary living in Madison and dating young executives, a dinner date was going to mean restaurants with plush carpet and dim lights and linen napkins tucked under rich silver forks, one for the salad and one for the meal.

But for now, this was it and this was him. Jens was fragrant with mouthwash and Mennen deodorant. He was wearing a thick cable-knit sweater and pressed slacks and a damped-down look of effort and polish. This date meant something to him; that realization steadied me.

We ordered from fake-leather menus: stuffed pork chops for me and rib-eye steak for him. The rib-eye was the most expensive dinner on the menu, and I had to wonder if that was to impress me. I sat back and smiled at him as the waitress left. It felt good to have someone trying to impress me.

Through most of the dinner we talked about Jens' plans for the future. He seemed to like his family's business well enough but didn't want to be stuck in Heron Lake all his life. His father owned a rather shabby fishing resort on the west shore: a dozen shingled cabins, boat dock and bait house and small café with gas pumps out front. I'd seen it from the road, and once our Luther League at church had rented a houseboat there for a party. Father had gone along to help.

When we'd finished eating we sat at the table as long as we could, talking. It was not yet eight, and my curfew was nine, so there was not enough time to do anything else, but too much time to go on sitting in a dining room where all the other tables were empty and the waitress was making pointed inquiries about whether or not we wanted anything else.

Finally we shifted to Jens' pickup truck, which was parked

in the small and very public lot behind the hotel. It was somewhat better than parking in the driveway at home, although I expected Father's headlights at any moment as he went to check the lock on the drug store.

"I really am sorry about my dad," I said as we settled into the cold cab of the pickup. Its faint fishy smell had survived weeks of winter. "Nine o'clock curfew must seem really insane to you. Now you know why I was never exactly in demand around school, for dating purposes."

He shrugged and twisted his long body to wedge between door and steering wheel, to look at me. "That's all right. You're worth it."

I felt like saying, how can you know what I'm worth? All we've talked about so far is you.

As though he'd heard me, he said, "So what are you going to do after graduation? You going to college or getting a job or what?"

"Getting away from home, mainly. If I can swing it. Not to college. That would take money. I'll just get a job, secretary probably at first till I can work up to something better."

He raised his eyebrows. "I figured you'd be going to college. You're smart enough, aren't you?"

I flushed at the question, and nodded. "But the problem is my father. His plan for me is to stay home, work in the store with him, and that's it. Period."

"What, be a pharmacist, you mean?"

Open your ears, dummy, I thought. "No, not as a pharmacist. That would take college and I just told you he's not letting me out of his sight for that long. He just wants me to clerk in the store all my life."

Jens snorted. "He can't do that. This is the nineteen-eighties. He can't make you stay home if you don't want to.

49

You can just take off after graduation and go get a job somewhere. No problem."

I shook my head. My neck was stiffening, talking sideways. "It's not that easy. I don't have any money nor any way of getting some. I could run away, maybe hitchhike to Madison or Chicago or someplace big enough to hide in, but what would I live on till I got a job?"

"You must have some money," he scoffed. I shook my head.

"Nor any way to get some. We don't have any close family. The only friend I have is Marlee Estes—you know, she works in the store—and she needs every penny she can scrape together for her college tuition."

I started to tell him about the cache of money in Marlee's care, but I wasn't sure enough yet that he could be trusted.

"Well," he said, "something will work out. You're a beautiful girl, Ariel. Somebody's going to come along and snatch you up." He smiled then, and pulled me to him.

For a first kiss, it wasn't a heavenly experience. My arm got hung up in the steering wheel, and his teeth were sharp ridges against my lip. He cradled my head in the hollow of his neck and stroked my hair, making it crackle and fly with electricity.

If the kiss was a disappointment, the closeness wasn't. With my face against his shoulder he became a blurred entity, no mouthwash breath or receding hairline, no slowness to understand my feelings. There was just the incredible luxury of being warmly held and stroked. Cared for.

Until that moment I hadn't recognized the strength of my hunger for the affectionate touch of another human being.

10

It was on the afternoon of New Year's Eve that things began unraveling. Mother and I and our minister's wife were unloading party supplies from the back of Pastor Bergman's station wagon, at the side door of the church.

Peace Lutheran was the newest and wealthiest church of the three in town, a low, red brick building with a modern concrete cross in front and neatly trimmed shrubbery. It stood on a corner where the business district met a street of big old houses, well kept and placid.

The station wagon was parked in the alley that led to the parking lot behind the church. The church's side door, which was propped open for our cartons, led directly downstairs to the fellowship room in the basement. Mother and I and a dozen other volunteers were putting up decorations that afternoon for the Luther League New Year's Eve party.

The idea behind the party was to keep the church's youth safe and sober on that dangerous night each year, and of course each year it failed. The kids who most needed to be kept safe would rather be whipped naked through the streets than be seen at a church party on New Year's Eve. The ones who did come, like Robin and me, were in no danger in the first place.

For the Brecht girls, of course, there was no choice. Father was the chairman of the committee, he and Mother chaperoned every year, and since we girls couldn't be left home unguarded on such a wild night, we came to the church party. Period.

This year, though, it wasn't going to be pure boredom. This year I was going with a date. When Jens asked me out for New Year's Eve, Father said it was the church party or nothing, and to my surprise Jens went along with it.

Father even brought home a new dress for me from Fashion Mart, and one for Robin. I'd have preferred picking mine out myself, but I could find no real fault with his choice, a champagne beige sweater dress with a fancy seed-pearl collar, removable for school wear. The fit was good, the color was perfect for my hair and skin, and it was exactly the right sort of dress for a church party, slightly dressy but totally modest. Robin's was similar, in a soft blue-green.

As I'd snipped off the labels, making the dress permanently mine, I had a sudden uncomfortable feeling that by accepting the dress, the gift of the dress, I was in some obscure way giving Father permission to dominate me. I should have refused to wear it, as Robin was doing. She hadn't cut the tags off hers. She was fighting him openly, and I wondered whether her way might not be healthier than mine. Safer in the long run.

Mrs. Bergman had already disappeared into the church with her load, and I was piling Mother's arms with bags of crepe-paper streamers when a familiar voice said, "There's Ariel."

I turned and froze. Mrs. Staas and Jason were on the sidewalk, Jason pulling his mother's shopping cart, one of those fold-down ones for old ladies who can't drive to the store. The Staases detoured toward Mother.

Mrs. Staas said, "I just wanted to tell you how much Jason enjoyed his lessons with Ariel. She helped him so much. Neither Jack nor I knew the first thing about skis, but Jason wanted a pair, so of course Santa had to bring him some, but if it hadn't been for Ariel teaching him, I don't think he'd ever have enjoyed it. Now he can't wait to get out on them."

My mind raced. As long as nothing was said about the money, I could just pass it off as helping a little kid do a few things on his skis.

Mother looked faintly nonplussed but said, "Well, that's nice to hear. I'm glad Ariel could be of some help. I'm sure she enjoyed it, too."

To me, Mrs. Staas said, "I'm sorry we can't afford to go on paying you for regular lessons, Ariel, but I think he's got enough of a start now so that he can go out with his friends and keep up pretty well. If you'd sort of keep an eye out for him, maybe go along with him from time to time, we'd really appreciate it. From the way Jason jabbered about you, you really made a hit with him. You remember I told you, years ago when you were in my class, that you should think about teaching as a career."

Mother said, "Frank wants Ariel to go into the store with him after she graduates." Her voice carried a note of pride, of family solidarity.

When Mrs. Staas was gone, Mother turned to me, more puzzled than angry. "What did she mean about paying you?"

Mrs. Bergman emerged, puffing from the climb up the stairs, and relieved Mother of the bags of streamers. "Come on, Judith, these things aren't going to hang themselves. You should see what they've done with the bulletin boards. . . ." Her voice faded as she sensed the quiet between Mother and me.

A decision hardened in me. To Mrs. Bergman I said, "We'll be down in a few minutes. We just need to talk about something for a second, okay?"

I slammed down the tailgate and, of one accord, Mother and I climbed into the car's back seat and hunched within our coats. She waited silently for me to begin.

"I have been keeping this from you and Father," I began slowly. "I did give Jason a few lessons and I did charge for them, and I did keep the money. I did it for a reason, and I know I'm taking a huge chance here, asking you to keep a secret from him."

Her face was still, expressionless. It was a soft, round colorless face, papery in texture, brows almost invisibly pale, like mine. This face was so familiar to me that I could barely see it. It was a face that smiled easily, but not as Marlee's did, from the joy of her nature. Mother's smiles were based on insecurity, anxiety to give to everyone what was wanted. Fear of disapproval, even from her children. This was not the enemy, I knew. And yet, I doubted there was enough strength left in her to make her a reliable ally. Still, I had no choice now.

I pulled in a long breath and said, "Mother, I have to get away from here. As soon as graduation is over, I have to leave here and get a job someplace. Now, I don't know yet how I'm going to swing it, but I do know it's going to take some money, and that's why I charged the Staases for Jason's

54

lessons and hid the money. I'm not asking you to help me, because I know you don't have any money either or any way of getting any. All I'm asking is for you not to tell him. Just give me my chance, will you?"

Her eyes had darkened and widened when I said "leave." She stared at me now. "But your father wants you to work in the store with him, Arie. You know that."

"Of course I know it! He's been saying it for years. But Mother! That's not the life I want for myself. I hate him. You must know Robin and I hate him. He treats us like prisoners. All of us, you too. Surely you don't like living this way any more than we do." She didn't answer. "Do you?" I insisted.

"Your father takes very good care of us," she said faintly. "You girls don't appreciate the things he does. . . ."

"Mother, come on. The man is not normal, mentally. You're married to him. You must know that. You don't think it's normal the way he controls every detail of our lives, never letting us handle money, or go out after dark, or use the phone. He's sick."

Her skin flushed dull red at the neck but whitened at the root of her nose. "You must never say things like that. He is your father. He loves you girls, and everything he does is to protect you."

"No, Mother. Everything he does is to punish us. For some twisted reason he has to control us absolutely, and at the same time he has to look like Superfather to everybody else in this town. And the hell of it is he gets away with it. Did you know I tried to talk to the school counselor about him when I was in eighth grade? You know what she said? She said that as long as he wasn't physically abusing Robin and me, there was nothing she could do about it."

She said nothing, just looked at me from behind those expressionless eyes.

More quietly I went on. "I don't know what century he thinks he's living in, but Mom, how can he honestly think he can own Robin and me so completely? Doesn't he realize that Robin's going to run away as soon as she can manage it? And that he can't force me to stay at home and work in the store if I don't want to?"

She shook her head gently; I couldn't tell what she was denying.

"Mom, I'm not asking you to do anything against him, lie to him or anything like that. All I'm asking is that you don't tell him about the Jason money. It's only sixty dollars, and it's probably not even enough to get away on, but it's all I'm ever likely to have in the way of . . . a chance. Just don't take that away from me by telling him, okay?"

She said nothing.

"Okay, Mother? Will you do that?"

"I don't know, Ariel. He just wants you to stay home where you'll be safe. I want you to be safe, too. I don't know what's right or wrong in this."

"You've been married to him too long." My voice hardened. "You don't have any opinions of your own any more."

From the church door Mrs. Bergman yelled cheerfuly, "Come on, you two. We need Ariel on the stepladder."

We climbed out of our opposite doors without looking at each other again.

56

11

The party turned out better than I'd hoped. I forced myself to block out the worry about Mother and to enjoy the feel of the new dress without thinking about who had provided it or what the ultimate price might be. The nubbly knit felt good against my calves, and the color made my skin more ivory than pasty.

Jens called for me, made polite conversation with Father for a few minutes, then handed me up into his fish-fragrant pickup cab. My family followed, Father's headlights never out of Jens's rearview mirror.

We were early, but the awkward time was absorbed by kitchen jobs. In the long bright kitchen at one end of the fellowship hall, Jens cheerfully filled pretzel bowls for Mrs. Bergman. While I rinsed and dried punch cups, dusty from a year of disuse, my eyes followed Jens, studied him.

Was it possible that Jens Jensen was going to be my Manifest Destiny? He seemed so at home with my family, in my

57

church basement. I remembered Robin saying, "Marry him. It's a way out," and I pondered . . .

The fellowship hall was a huge bare room with green tile floors and paler green concrete-block walls. Folding chairs and long brown Masonite tables lined the walls, and our paper streamers tented out from the central light fixture, red and white twisted together. With care, they could be used again for the Valentine's dance.

Gradually the room filled as junior high and high school kids arrived in clots of three or four. Few came with dates; the daters were at better parties or out on their own. There were almost as many sets of parents around the edges as there were Luther Leaguers. Typical.

We danced to records played on a portable stereo. The room was too bright and too big, too empty of kids and too full of smiling, watching parents. But Jens drew me onto the floor, and gradually others followed. I liked him for doing that. It took a special kind of courage to be the first on the dance floor.

I wasn't very good at the dancing, but he worked around my awkwardness until it faded. He grinned and joked with passing dancers and so obviously enjoyed himself that my ineptness wasn't important.

On the slow-dance numbers he held me just close enough, for a church dance with parents watching. But I felt the warmth of him, and the trembling of his hand on my back. He was getting more out of this than could be seen from Father's viewpoint. At carefully chosen moments, when Father couldn't see us, Jens would lower his face to brush against my hair and murmur, "You're my beautiful blonde."

There was no chance to hide at midnight for the special kiss because we all had to join in a circle of fellowship in the center of the room, with our arms crossed in front of us and hands clasped around the ring. Pastor Bergman said a quick prayer, which probably even he didn't listen to. Then with laughter and release, the party was over.

We were expected to stay and help with the cleanup, but Jens was quicker than Father, and had our coats and our escape well in hand while Father was still stage-managing the gathering of paper plates and punch cups.

"We'll have to be home before they get there," I said, breathless with the run toward the pickup.

"I know, but we can have a little time alone anyhow."

He drove as fast as he could get away with, and parked in front of our house.

"Now," he said, and kissed me seriously. "Happy New Year, my beautiful blonde. May we be together for many more."

It was the kind of thing people say on New Year's Eve. It didn't mean anything serious, and I wasn't sure I wanted it to, but the romance of it was like helium in my head.

"You are my girl, and no one else's, right?" he said, holding my face between his hands.

"Yes." I didn't want to belong to him. I was fighting with everything in me to belong to no one but myself. But the gentleness of him was balm to a lifetime of wounds, and I told him what he wanted to hear.

Just as my mother did with my father.

12

Into the blackness of my bedroom Father crashed, bringing light and noise. I sat up, terrified, my pulse hammering in my neck.

"You little liar," he screamed. "Hiding money from me. Where is it? Where did you hide it? You're not getting away with this, you little sneak. I don't raise lying, sneaking daughters. I want that money and I want it right now."

Like an enraged dog, he seemed to swell in size. I huddled in my bed, staring at his reddened face. Without his glasses, he seemed alien and oddly off balance, blurred as the world looked blurred to him. At his temple an artery swelled and throbbed.

I was disoriented. It was black night and I had been deep in sleep, but I dared not take my eyes away from him to glance at the clock. She told him, I thought. She must have told him in bed, after they got home from church.

"I didn't do anything wrong," I tried gallantly. It would be no use, of course.

"Nothing wrong!" His voice rose and split into a duet. For an instant I imagined him crumpling beside my bed with a stroke or a heart attack. There was no time to react to that possibility.

"Nothing wrong? You hire yourself out as some kind of ski instructor when you hardly know how to ski yourself. You have the gall to charge for your services like some prostitute. You take sixty dollars from good people like the Staases. What did you do, tell them your father is too cheap to give you spending money? Huh? Huh, Missy? Is that what you told them?"

"No. I didn't tell them anything."

I looked behind him to see if Mother was in the hallway, but it was only Robin.

Father snapped, "Go back to your room, Robin. This is no business of yours."

He was in his pajamas, white cotton with a blue-stripe pattern and dangling drawstrings at the waist. His ankles and feet were bare blue-white skin, hairless and corded with veins. The big-toe nails were long, curved horny things as yellow as the calluses beside them.

I hated him deeply and purely.

His voice grew quieter, but sharp. "I want that money right now, Ariel. You get up out of that bed and give it to me. I know it's in this room somewhere."

Panic fluttered in my stomach. If he found out Marlee was helping me in this, she would lose her job. In a town the size of Heron Lake, jobs for high school girls were impossible to find. She was still four hundred dollars short of her first year's tuition and dorm fees, and hadn't even started on textbook money.

Holding my nerve together, I faced him down. "I'll give it to you tomorrow, but I can't get it now. I hid it outside."

"Liar," he spat. New rage flared behind his puffy eyes. He spun and jerked the top drawer out of my dresser. Panties and bras and a Tampax box arced through the air. He dove into the things, scattering them, touching them. I shuddered. I'd have to wash everything before I could stand to put it on. Out came the second drawer. Pajamas, scarves, knee socks. The pile on the floor grew. He ripped the newspaper linings out of the drawers, searched the underside of each drawer. The third one: sweaters, swim suit, ski underwear. Not so bad now. I could stand this.

Then the closet. He ripped everything from the hangers, jammed his fingers into shoes and boots. On it went, all the way around the room, boxes and picture frames and throw rugs. When he got to the bed I stood up, stood aside while he stripped off sheets and mattress pad and pillow cases, then hauled the mattress itself off the springs.

When he finished he was spent and the room was a tornado path. He looked at me.

Carefully, trying not to enflame him again, I repeated, "I hid it outside and I'll give it to you in the morning, as soon as it gets light enough to find it."

His breath was shallow and quick. He wanted to hit me; I could feel his hatred from six feet away. His fingers bent as though they had my neck within them. I wanted him to attack me. I wanted to fight him and hurt him and get this out in the open. I wanted him to put wounds on me that I could show to the town. Here is your model father, Heron Lake. Here is Frank Brecht, pillar of the church, big man in Rotary and Chamber of Commerce and every other damned thing in this town. Look at him now, and see if you believe Robin and me.

Sanity flickered again in his eyes. Caution. With a wave of his arm at the wreckage, he said, "Clean this up," and went down the stairs to his waiting wife.

I made enough noise putting back drawers and mattress to cover the sound of Robin's scurry across the hall. She closed my door behind her and stared around, awed at the mess. Our eyes met across the mattress.

As she helped me shove the unwieldy mattress into place, I puffed, "Listen. I need you. Can you get out of the house?"

"Sure." She had a back-porch roof beneath one window.

"Go over to Marlee's, wake her up, get my sixty dollars, tell her what happened. Stick it . . ."

We thought.

"The bird house," I said.

She shook her head. "I can't reach up that high."

I thought again. "I know. Up under the eaves of the back-porch roof, at that east corner, you know, the wasp nest?"

Her eyes widened.

"They're not alive in winter," I said. "Just wad it up and stick it behind the wasp nest. You can reach that if you stand on the rail."

She nodded, memorizing her instructions as she slipped out into the darkened hallway. I gave her a few minutes to dig some kind of warm clothing out of her closet, since downstairs was impossible. Then I made noise again, shoving my desk back into place to cover her exit from the porch roof.

I lay stiffly in my re-made bed, watching the slow progress of the numbers on my digital clock radio and imagining Robin running down Pine, across Second, up Shore to 319.

Knocking on Marlee's door and waking the family. Explaining, apologizing, running back.

What a sister. She almost made up for the rest of the family.

Forty-one minutes later I heard the faint scraping of her window, and the soft clump of a boot being shucked. A few minutes later her bare feet padded past my door and into the bathroom. That was to let me know she was back. I got up and went to the bathroom door and called softly, "Are you okay?" Innocent sisterly question.

"Fine. Everything's fine," she said. Innocent sisterly reassurance.

It wasn't until we were both in bed again and the worst of the crisis was over that I realized the enormity of my loss.

Sixty dollars wouldn't have gone very far, but it would have been, barely, enough of a wing to fly on.

Now there was nothing.

13

January was an endless, dreadful month. My punishment for the Jason lessons was a month of being grounded. By Father's definition, that meant that I remained within his sight every minute I wasn't actually in school. He drove me and Robin the eight blocks to school every morning, and he left the store in Mrs. Krischner's hands every afternoon to pick me up and bring me to the store. Mrs. Krischner was his daytime clerk, whom Marlee replaced after school because Mrs. Krischner needed to be at home when her own children got there.

I spent the late afternoons in the back room of the store doing my homework on the scarred old desk where Mrs. Krischner did the store's bookkeeping. There was no skiing, even on weekends, and of course there were no dates with Jens.

It was understood between Father and me that the matter was not to be talked about around school. Everyone thought

65

he was being a wonderful, thoughtful father, saving me a cold walk every afternoon. Robin may have told a few people, I don't know. To me it didn't seem worth the effort. People had tended not to believe me when I'd tried to describe Father in the past. They probably wrote me off as a rebellious teenager, just exaggerating her gripes.

Two or three days a week Marlee lent me quarters to call Jens during the noon hour. He couldn't talk much in front of his family, nor could I in the noisy hall outside the school cafeteria. But it was contact of sorts, and we had to make do with it. Father always answered the phone at home, and he'd curtly cut off Jens' early attempts to bridge the blockade.

The first Saturday, Father took me to the store with him, to spend the day clerking with Marlee. The time dragged incredibly. Being with Marlee would have been fun if it hadn't been for that green-coated figure standing in his raised and lighted cubicle at the end of the dim store, watching us. The store had few customers, even on Saturdays. Almost everything it offered could be bought more conveniently at the Hy-Vee, or more cheaply at the K-Mart in Stevens Point, where much of Heron Lake went on Saturdays for serious shopping. The pharmacy counter was fairly busy, with elderly people buying prescriptions to treat winter colds and flu. But that was Father's bailiwick. Marlee and I dusted shelves of aspirin boxes that didn't need dusting, and stood around.

When I thought about spending my one and only life in this dingy brown store, under Father's eye, I wanted to scream.

But after that first Saturday, he left me at home, with Mother to prevent my going out or making phone calls. That was only a little less awful, because I could not forgive her for betraying me to him.

And God punished me further by sending beautiful sunny Saturdays, when I ached to be out on the trails, skimming the wind on my Gazelles and talking to real-live people at the warming hut. Jens especially.

Within my pressurized captivity I lived for the final escape. With the Jason money gone it might mean begging from Jens or even from strangers, but it was going to happen. The aching of my earlier escape-dreams was hardening now into iron resolve.

I began sewing on those interminable weekends. I took apart an outgrown wool skirt and made a vest from it. Swallowing my distaste, I asked Father to take me to the fabric store in Stevens Point on Thursday evening when the stores stayed open late. He waited near the cash register and cheerfully paid for everything I bought: skirt lengths of washable wool, a pattern, and brown corduroy for a shirt dress, and from the remnant tables enough summer-weight knits for several outfits.

He didn't know it, but he was paying for a secretary's wardrobe, not a store clerk's.

For a while Robin and I talked about the possibility of selling some of these new clothes to kids at school. It would be easy enough to wear two layers of clothes out of the house and to leave the money in my locker at school. But I couldn't quite bring myself to approach anyone with such a humiliating suggestion. And Father might be keeping track of the sewing projects.

Oddly, as the month progressed and my hatred toward him compacted, Father seemed to mellow toward me. It was as if,

67

having made me his chained fox, he was determined to make a pet of me. He smiled, he spoke more warmly to me than I'd ever remembered, and in the car in the evenings, driving home from the store, he talked.

"That Stuart ought to give up his practice. The man is so senile he can't even find his stethoscope hanging around his neck."

Within the privacy of our family I had never heard my father say one positive thing about any of the three doctors in town. He himself had wanted to be a doctor but had had neither the money nor the grades to get into med school. Marlee thought he was full of envy and frustration toward doctors in general, and she was probably right. He was always arrogant in his derision of their prescription habits.

Now, he somehow seemed to assume that I was on his team. It was unsettling, the way he radiated affection toward me once I was totally within his power. It made me wonder again about Mother. Had she been lulled and trained this way, as a seventeen-year-old bride? Go against me and I'll humiliate you; give in to me and I'll reward you with affection.

My anger toward her for betraying me gradually subsided into a kind of pity, a sadness for the woman she might have grown into, married to a normal man.

During that long January I took thoughts of Jens to bed with me. I lay in the dark, with my bedside radio playing softly, and remembered how it felt to sink against his warmth in the pickup, the gentleness of his fingertips stroking back my hair. Gradually, he grew better looking, more intelligent, more sensitive as the nights and their imaginings passed.

January twenty-seventh was Robin's fifteenth birthday. Father took us out to dinner at the Antlers and had the cook serve a surprise birthday cake and carry it, with candles lighted, through the restaurant to our table. His gift to her was an expensive cashmere sweater like a pink cloud. She was sullen through the cake presentation, obviously shrugging it off as grandstanding for the other people in the restaurant. But at the sight of the sweater, she cracked a little. When she thanked him it sounded almost genuine.

I went into her room that night just before lights-out, and caught her in the sweater and panties, looking at her top half in the mirror. I stretched across the bed and said, "It's a nice present."

"They all are." Her voice was clipped and hard.

"For a while there I thought you might be softening toward him. Have you noticed how nice he's being to me lately?"

She turned and gave me a look. "Sure. He thinks he's got you beat. Just try crossing him again and watch the fangs grow out."

She picked up a tall glass jar from the windowsill and held it toward the lamp. Inside was a twig with a gray cocoon, the size of a thumb, attached to it. For a long time she stared at the cocoon, as though she were sending silent messages to the embryo moth inside. Then, abruptly, she set the jar down and pulled the sweater off over her head.

"You're going to wear it, aren't you?" I asked. "That's too good a sweater to let go to waste just because of who gave it to you."

"I'll wear it when I leave this hell-hole," she said grimly.

14

Things eased a little in February. Robin was spending more and more time at Amy Stendorf's house in the evenings. That was allowable because Father could watch her all the way there and back from our living room window. I was back on my skis every afternoon between school and dark, and for long sweet silent times on weekends.

Jens and I began a routine of Friday and Saturday night dates, always within the bounds of Father's approval. He rather liked Jens, I'm not sure why, and he seemed to trust Jens to bring me back by ten on our date nights and to take me only to the pre-approved movies or basketball games.

On Valentine's Day, Jens gave me a sweetheart ring, a tiny gold heart with a chip of red stone in the center. I'd seen rings like it at K-Mart and I knew it hadn't cost much, but that was fine with me. I slipped it on my right hand ring finger and kissed him warmly in thanks. The ring made me feel tangibly valued.

We were in the truck, in the parking lot of the bowling alley, when he gave it to me. Two of his friends were meeting us there at seven, to bowl, and we were deliberately early.

Jens fingered the ring, twisting it on my bony hand. Then he picked up my left hand and pointedly plucked up the bare ring finger. "Would you wear it on this hand?"

I shook my head. "My father might think it meant . . . something more than just a sweetheart ring."

He gave me a deep long stare and said, "Would you like it to mean more?"

I looked away, not knowing how to answer that.

"Would you?" he pressed.

"Would I what?"

"You know."

Is this a proposal? I wondered frantically.

He held up my chin with his finger and smiled down into my eyes. "My beautiful blonde," he said.

I pulled away, mildly irritated. Every time he said that he made me feel abstract. I wasn't Ariel Brecht, individual; I was Jens Jensen's blonde.

His friends drove up then, and we all went inside. I'd never been bowling before, so the three of them had the fun of looking through the balls for one that fit me and teaching me how to count my steps and follow through on my swing. I caught on faster than they'd expected me to, and that was my evening's satisfaction.

The friends, Scott and Doug, were both out of high school and working around town somewhere, one in a garage and I wasn't sure about the other one. I wasn't entirely sure which was Scott and which was Doug; they were both short and dark and stocky and not the cleanest guys I'd ever seen. And

71

they each put away a six-pack of beer during the two hours we bowled.

All through the evening my attention followed Jens. He was different tonight. Our other dates had been solitary or with my family on New Year's Eve. This was the first time I'd seen him with his friends. He was louder and looser, which was understandable. He was also bossier.

It was obvious that he loved being the one with the girl. The blonde. Every time I walked close to him in the curved-bench area of our lane, he touched me in some proprietary way. I'd have enjoyed it if it had been directed at me and not at his audience.

Still, it was a fun evening. The racket of balls thudding, pins crashing, and voices shrilling was a lovely counterpoint to the month of silence at home with Father. Here, there was smoky air and beer cans on the table and laughter. Life.

We left at nine and drove to a spot along a side street where we could park publicly enough to look innocent, but more privately than in the driveway at home.

"What would you think about getting married?" Jens asked as soon as we'd warmed each other.

"Who, you and me?" I stalled for time.

"Of course, fluffhead. I'm not exactly proposing yet. I just wondered how you might feel about it if we did decide to."

I shook my head. "I don't want to get locked into anything like that yet. And I don't want to stay in this town."

"We wouldn't have to stay here, though. That's the thing." His voice gathered excitement. "We'd go to Madison. I'd go to school there, get my teaching degree so I could coach. You'd get a job and support us till I was out of school. That'd work just fine."

72

I pulled back and cocked my head to study him. Was he serious?

"I love you, Blondie," he said softly.

My eyes teared. There they were, the big words. He pulled me close and said into my hair, "You love me too, don't you?"

"Yes," I whispered, betraying every atom of myself. He wanted to hear it and I longed to say it to someone.

"Should we think about getting married then?"

I stiffened a little and shook my head against his sweater. "That's too fast, darling." I'd never tried an endearment before. It felt fake coming out of my mouth.

"That's okay." He rubbed the back of my neck with his long fingers. "We've got till spring to decide. I'll have to have college applications in by that time, and it'll be harder for me to get accepted since I've skipped a year of school. But we could get married right after you graduate and then stay here at my folks' through the summer, both of us working and saving money. And then move down to Madison in the fall."

A distortion of my escape plan, I thought. My vision was of solitary freedom, my own tiny apartment, a pleasant job in a friendly office, and, twice a month, paychecks in my absolute control. Dates. Skiing weekends with friends from the office. A perfect life that could go on until I fell strongly in love and wanted marriage, or until the time was right to make the move into a profession—architecture or design drafting or whatever it was going to be.

That dream floated like a silvery blue hot-air balloon on the horizon.

But here, within breathing distance was another dream, an

73

easier one. Not what I wanted, but what I could probably have.

I sat up straight and said seriously, "Jens, let me ask you something. If I said no about the marriage, would you still be my friend? I mean, would you be willing to help me get what I really want?"

"What's that?"

"You know. We've talked about it before. I want to go away on my own after graduation, get a job and live alone for a while. It's important to me. But I can't swing it without help. Would you drive me to Madison or somewhere, and would you lend me enough money to live on till I could get a job?"

"Hell, no," he yelped. "I want you here with me. Why would I help you get away from me? And what's the big deal about living alone? Why would you want to live alone when we could get married and have each other? We could apply for married-students' housing on campus, cheaper than an apartment in town. It'd be fun."

It would be a way out. Something in me cringed at the thought of living in close quarters with Jens, but it would be a step up from life at home.

As we drove home I considered telling Robin about all this. She'd be against it, I knew. There wouldn't be room in student housing for an extra sister, and I knew she was hanging on by her fingernails, counting on following me out of here this summer.

When we turned the corner onto Pine, I sat upright, away from Jens. In front of our house was a police car idling silently but with its light turning, throwing blue and white circles across the houses nearby.

Our porch lights were blazing, and neighbors watched

from their front doors. I ran inside with Jens striding behind me. Suicide. For some reason I was sure it was Robin or Mother, dead.

Mother was upright, in the hall with Father and Ed Lasky, our night cop. Robin then, I thought wildly.

I couldn't pull in enough breath to ask. Father swept Jens out the door, saying it was a small family matter. Private.

To me he said, "Ariel, you no longer have a sister."

"Dead?" I gasped.

He shook his head. "Unfortunately she is not dead. She has run away."

I sagged in relief.

He went on. "She's run away with Lyle Stendorf."

I stared blankly at him, at Mother. Who was Lyle. . . ?

"You mean Mr. Stendorf? Amy's father?"

Father's blank hard eyes answered me.

15

Of course it was all over school by Monday. With his initial
fury that drove him to call the police, Father had blown away
all hope of hiding Robin's escape.

He'd gone across the street to the Stendorfs' around nine-
thirty, because Robin was supposed to have been home by
nine. What he found, instead of a tardy daughter, was Mrs.
Stendorf sitting dazed at the kitchen table holding a note in
her hand. She and Amy had left after school to drive to Fond
du Lac, to leave Amy for the weekend at her grandparents'.
Mr. Stendorf had told her he had to work that evening.

I wasn't surprised that Robin had run away; she'd been
near the boiling point all winter. But with Mr. Stendorf? He
was old enough to be her . . . ah, of course. Her father. He
had probably just been nice to her in the beginning, and with
her passion for pain she had demanded more. I felt terribly
sorry for Mrs. Stendorf and for Amy, who would have to hear
the whispers at school. But for Robin, something inside me

cheered. She might have done it in a stupid, hurtful way, but she had made her move.

All through the weekend, Father alternately raged and held himself above rage. He disowned her, he made wild threats of punishment for her when he got her home. By Sunday he was talking more and more as though I were now his only living daughter. I felt nets closing in on me.

On Monday afternoon the highway patrol called Father at the store. Robin was in Milwaukee, alone. She'd been picked up from a downtown sidewalk at one in the morning by a suspicious cruising patrol car, and they were holding her in a juvenile-detention center.

I wasn't there when the call came, but Marlee told me what he'd said. "Leave her in jail. She can rot there." But apparently that was only a first reaction, or else the police had refused to keep her and had insisted on his coming to get her. At any rate, by the time he got home from the store, his rejection had softened. He would leave her in jail overnight and go after her in the morning.

Mother wanted to go that night, but he said no, it would do her good to be uncomfortable for one night, after the hell she'd put the family through for three days.

"What happened to Mr. Stendorf?" I asked. It seemed to be the logical question. No one knew. Father hadn't thought to ask.

He left at seven the next morning. Knowing he was out of Heron Lake, I did something I'd never even considered before. I dressed in warm hiking clothes and skipped school. Mother was in such a snit about Robin she didn't even notice the sweat pants and high woolly boots and ski jacket.

It was two miles around the lake to Jens' camp by road, but less than half a mile by ice, straight across the lake. I trudged out, past the miniature huts of half a dozen ice fishermen, feeling exposed to every pair of eyes in town, and not caring.

It was a raw, windy day, with low tattered clouds full of snow waiting to fall. I hunched my shoulders around my ears, jammed fists into pockets, and plodded. I needed somebody of my own to talk to. Marlee would have been better, but to get to her I'd have had to face school, and I needed to get away from all those people saying, "Heard anything from Robin yet?"

It was an easy step up from the lake's ice onto the ramshackle boat dock at the Hideaway. No one was around the boat sheds or bait-shop area, even though there had been a few ice fishermen out huddling over their black, sawn holes near the dock. Between shore and the main building were a dozen rustic rental shacks, also looking deserted. Only the main building showed lights.

It was a flat-roofed, two-story box, café and cabin-rental office downstairs, family living quarters upstairs. Jens had brought me out for a quick look around on one of our earlier dates. Behind the main building and up a steep hill was the blacktop road that circled the lake.

There were lights on in the café, although no cars stood in the parking area. I pushed in the door, stamping the snow from my boots. Now that I was here, I didn't know why I'd come.

Jens' mother sat on a high stool behind the counter, drinking coffee and reading the morning paper. She was a big-boned hefty woman with chapped cheeks and pale hair flying wildly from an up-folded knot at the back of her head. Jens told me she had it done once a week in town and never touched it between times.

"Well look what the wind blew in," she said, laying down her paper.

"Is Jens around?"

"What'd you do, walk all the way over here? You must be froze to a frizz. Pull up here under the blower."

She sat me directly beneath a brown metal air duct that parted my hair with its hot breath. "Jens," she bellowed up the stairs behind the counter, and in one long motion poured me a cup of coffee.

I shook my head, but she said, "On the house. You need it. It's two above, out there. Got down to nine below overnight, said on the radio this morning. Heard anything from your sis yet?"

No secrets in Heron Lake.

Jens came shambling down the stairs, snapping his jeans and yawning. He'd been in bed, obviously.

"Arie. What are you doing here?"

I decided I liked his mother's greeting better. He yawned again and scratched himself and bent to give me a quick kiss. His breath smelled awful. I ducked away and glanced at his mother, embarrassed.

"How come you're not at school?" Jens asked as he accepted a coffee cup from his mother. "Hand over those rolls, would you?" She slid him a plate of stale-looking restaurant rolls, flat disks with white icing and raisins. I shook my head at them, but drank my coffee. Its heat outweighed its bitterness.

"They found Robin last night," I told him.

"Is she all right?"

I liked him for asking that first, ahead of all the other ques-

79

tions. He probably was a perfectly nice guy, I told myself. Anyone can have bad breath when they first get up.

"She's in Milwaukee. Okay, as far as I know. The police picked her up walking around downtown in the middle of the night. Father went to get her today."

"What about her boyfriend?" Mrs. Jensen asked. She'd gone back to her paper with her eyes, but not her ears.

"Mr. Stendorf?" I asked stupidly.

She nodded.

"I don't know." I shrugged. "Nobody said anything about him."

"Probably dumped her," the woman said, and made a face into her cooling coffee.

The café was a single square room with large windows on the two sides that faced the lake. Six small tables took up most of the floor space. The walls were high-gloss knotty pine, covered with four-by-twelve-inch cartoon cards, most of them dirty. There were a few mounted fish, photographs of more dead fish, and notices of farm auctions. On a bulletin board near the door were dozens of smaller notices, hand printed: Custom Bulldozing And Backhoe Work, Chest-Type Freezer For Sale; Free Kittens To Good Homes. The glass case under the cash register held cheap billed caps saying Hideaway Resort, small pine plaques saying I Only Go Fishing For The Halibut, and Fishermen Have A Better Line.

The place fit Jens. Watching him slouch around his coffee cup I had a sudden vision of him sitting right there, years later.

And me? If I did marry him, is this where my life would be played out, in this square fishy pine room? Behind the counter, waiting on customers? I shuddered.

80

Since I had nothing else to do for the rest of my hooky day, I stayed and relaxed into the warmth of the room. From time to time during the morning, one or two of the ice fishermen came in, bringing loud voices and cold air. No one sat separately, they all joined the three of us at the counter, or pulled their chairs around toward us in a visiting circle. No one seemed to have anything better to do with the morning than to drink cup after cup of coffee and talk endlessly about nothing.

Around noon a few more came in, and we all had cheeseburgers or greasy tenderloin sandwiches. At Mrs. Jensen's casual suggestion I took over the drowning of frozen French fries in a well of spitting brown fat.

After lunch Jens took me out for a walk around the place. He showed me the cabins, the boat house, and his own private johnboat, dark green and battered and unimpressive. He seemed to want me to like his world, so I said that's nice, this is nice. When he took me into an empty cabin and kissed me and told me he loved me, it really was nice. Until he tried to ease me toward the bed. I shied away, and he held me gently again, and apologized.

At about the time school got out, Jens drove me back to the edge of town in his truck, called me his very own beautiful blonde, and left me to walk innocently home from the direction of the school.

Father's car was in the driveway.

16

Father came down the front steps as I was going up. He gave me a hard look that I couldn't translate—don't be kind to your sister?—and went on toward the car, saying something about checking in at the store.

Mother was in the kitchen holding a package of paper-wrapped meat from the freezer and looking as if she'd forgotten what she had started to do with it.

"How's Robbie?"

She looked at me with brimming eyes and shook her head.

From upstairs I could hear bathwater running. I ran up and opened the bathroom door. Robin was lying in the tub, her arms floating on the rim-high water, her eyes closed. I turned off the faucet and dropped the toilet lid for a seat. As I settled with my feet on the tub, I was struck by the fact that she was still wearing her panties.

"Didn't you forget to take something off?" I asked in an attempt to sound normal and big-sisterish.

She opened her eyes but focused somewhere off my left shoulder. "It didn't work," she said dully.

"What? Your escape plan?"

She closed her eyes again.

"Well, what happened? Come on, tell me. I've been going out of my mind all weekend." I noticed the pile of clothes on the floor beside the tub, her favorite blue skirt and the pink cashmere sweater. She'd said she wouldn't wear it until she left here. She must have had it on through the whole awful experience, whatever that had been.

I prodded again. "What was the deal with Mr. Stendorf? Did you get him to take you someplace, or what?"

She nodded then and sat up a few inches. Slowly she ran the bar of soap up and down one arm. "Yeah. I thought he'd just take me to Milwaukee and give me enough money to live on till I could get a waitress job or something fast like that. I figured I'd luck onto some nice kids with their own apartment and crash with them a while, or something. I don't know. Something. I was so sure that if I could just get away from here I'd be able to get along one way or another."

"But what happened? How did you get him to take you? What happened to him?"

"I don't know how it got started," she sighed. "He was just always hanging around when I was over at Amy's, joking and kind of flirting, you know, not seriously. And then one time in the garage he kissed me. And I liked it, you know?" Her eyes met mine then, and begged for understanding. I nodded. I did know.

"So then we started messing around a little, you know, whenever no one was around. So finally I asked him if he'd help me get away, and he said sure, he'd do anything I wanted. He fixed it up so Mrs. Stendorf and Amy would be

83

going to Fond du Lac in her car Friday night, and I just went over there like I always did, and we got in the car and I bent way down so nobody could see me, and we went."

"So what happened?"

She shook her head and closed her eyes, and sank so low in the water that for a panicky instant I thought she was trying to drown herself. "Come on, Rob. You have to tell me. I'm not going to tell anybody, you know that. I'm on your side. But you'll feel better if you tell somebody."

She did sink all the way under then, but with her breath held, and when she broke the surface and blew out her breath, the words came too.

"He took me to this motel. Holiday Inn," she said bitterly. "I thought he was just going to leave me there and give me some money. Boy, was that ever dumb of me."

"He stayed with you?"

She nodded. "He started telling me I owed it to him, that he'd thrown away his marriage just for me, his wife would never forgive him for this, he loved me. All that junk. I kept telling him I didn't want to, but he got really mad, Arie."

My eyes widened. "Did he rape you?"

"No. Not exactly. I mean, I finally decided I really did owe him, for bringing me there and everything. And I figured he never would give me the money to live on, if I didn't do what he wanted."

We were silent then, while I imagined what poor Robbie must have gone through. She went on. "Well, after that I figured he'd stay with me, maybe get a divorce and marry me when I was old enough, or at least stay in Milwaukee with me and take care of me. But when I woke up in the morning he was gone. Nobody's seen him since."

"He probably got to thinking about going to jail for statutory rape, which is what he could be charged with, since you're only fifteen. Did he leave you any money?"

"No." Tears brimmed then. "He didn't even pay the motel bill. I didn't think the manager was ever going to let me out of there. He took Lyle's name and home address—I guess Lyle gave him a phony name when he checked in. So then I took off and started walking toward downtown. I couldn't think of anything else to do. The motel was way out somewhere along an interstate, but I could see where the main skyscrapers were, downtown."

"What did you do for food?"

"Starved. I did hitch a ride part of the way and the people had some doughnuts in the car, so I had three doughnuts, but that was all. So when I got downtown I just started wandering around. It was so huge. I couldn't believe it. I had no idea where I was or what direction I was going.

"I went in about eight or nine restaurants and asked for a job, but . . ." She shook her head. "One place said they'd try me, but I'd have to buy my own uniform before I could start, and they wouldn't advance me the money to buy it with. Another place started to hire me till they found out I wasn't living anywhere."

"So what did you do?"

She turned her face away from me. "I really don't want to talk about the rest of it, Arie, okay? It was so awful I can't even think about it."

"Did you live on the street?" I asked gently, awed at her experience.

"Something like that. I got down into this terrible part of town because it was the only place that seemed . . . warm. I could get a little food there anyhow, begging. And somebody took me home with him one night, I don't know who he was,

85

some kind of bum but he had a little room. He left me alone and let me sleep there for a while. It smelled awful. But when I went out again these women beat me up. Said they were going to beat me up, anyway. Pushed me around, and one of them had a knife. I kept expecting Dad to come along and get everything straightened out, you know?"

I was too full of feeling to speak.

"And then when the police finally found me I thought, good, now at least somebody will take care of me. Dad will come and get me. But he didn't, Arie."

"Yes he did. What are you talking about?"

"He told them to leave me in jail overnight and he'd come when he got around to it. He told them I was scum and I belonged in jail."

"Robin! He did not. He never said you were scum, or anything like it. I think he just wanted to teach you a lesson, leaving you there overnight."

Her eyes opened wide again and fastened onto mine. "He was too late. I already learned."

17

In March the earth reappeared in the ski tracks and melted outward toward the trees. With aching reluctance I hot-waxed the Gazelles and hung them up for the season.

Our lives settled into an uneasy normalcy. Robin was back in school, Jens and I were a steady couple with routine week-end dates, and Father had quit talking about filing charges against Mr. Stendorf. Mrs. Stendorf filed for divorce and moved to Fond du Lac, and some people from Waukesha bought their house.

I'm not sure how Robin faced everybody at school, that first day back, but somehow she got through it and settled back into the routine of her classes. Often I found myself studying my sister. There was an elemental change in her since the Milwaukee experience. Something had been destroyed in her, something extinguished. The hate seemed to have evaporated from her spirit, and it had been the hating that had fired and strengthened her.

Now, she seemed to have accepted Father's judgment of her worthlessness. She still talked spitefully about him when we were alone, but I noticed that it was always me who started those conversations, not Robin. She recited the old lines and played the part of rebellious daughter, but only in a wooden way.

As the weeks passed, I noticed something even more disturbing. Father was warming toward Robin. He drew her into conversations at the supper table, almost as though he were wooing her. He spoke in a gentler tone to her now and sometimes patted her shoulder in passing.

At times I thought he was mellowing at last and learning how to love his daughters in a normal way. But then I remembered that he treated me with this same gentleness during my month of punishment in January, when I was his captive, and I shivered in fear for Robin's future. Was she broken already, after one attempt at being her own person? Was his power that great and that insidious? And if tough little Robin was already defeated, what would happen to me if I tried for my own freedom and failed?

Once in late March, when I'd been stewing about my future and when Father seemed especially mellow, I tried again to talk to him. Mother had already gone up to bed, and he and Robin were just finishing a game of cribbage. I'd been watching the game idly, working up to what I wanted to say.

He gave me a perfect opening. "I had a talk with Marlee today," he said. "I told her I could keep her on at full salary through the summer, at least until August first. That will give you two months to learn her job while Mrs. Krischner is on vacation. You can be learning the bookkeeping end of it, too, and then Mrs. Krischner can go on part-time when school starts. I thought we might take a family vacation that first week in June, give you girls a break after your school year. We can get in someplace on Mackinac Island if we get our reservations in pretty soon now."

"Father, I don't want to work in the store. We've talked about this before, and you keep saying I have to, but I really honestly do not want to stay in Heron Lake after I get out of school."

His face darkened, and the artery above his temple began throbbing visibly. Robin got up and slipped silently up the stairs.

"I suppose you want to go off to Milwaukee and turn prostitute like your sister," he said in his metallic voice. I knew then that his new tenderness toward Robin had nothing to do with genuine feeling for her. He was the lion-tamer, she was the drugged and spiritless beast. Her weakness gave him the feeling of power he needed, and that was all there was between them. I shuddered.

"No, that's not what I want. I want to go to Madison, get a beginning secretarial job and a nice little apartment, and build a good life for myself, a good decent life, but where I'll have charge of myself. I need that. I'll never grow up unless I have that chance, Father."

He snorted and relaxed. His battle was already won. "Who'd hire you? You have no experience, no brains."

"I've been taking Typing and Computer and Business Skills. I've always gotten good grades in those classes, and I'm in my third year of typing. I can do sixty-three words a minute with no errors, I can compose the best business letters in the class, and my teacher says I'm definitely ready for an entry-level job anywhere."

He snorted and waved away my qualifications. "High school classes. You don't think anyone in his right mind

89

would hire you. And you could never make it on your own even if you did get a job. You don't know the first thing about handling money."

"Well, whose fault is that?" I yelled.

He stared me down. His eyes behind the smudgy glasses were marbles set in dough. There was no emotion behind them, no flicker of humanity.

Carefully, as though speaking to an idiot, he said, "Ariel, you are my responsibility. You saw what happened to your sister when she tried to get along without me. You are certainly no better than she is. I will not have you living in some filthy city, taking drugs and sleeping with whatever man wants you."

My mouth gaped open.

"You will stay here in your home where I can protect you from things you know nothing about. You will work in the store where I can make sure nothing will hurt you. You will live here in your own home like a decent young woman. And that's the end of it."

When I went upstairs I heard Robin moving quickly toward her room. She'd been listening at the top of the stairs. I followed her.

She was sitting at her desk, idly balancing the jar with the moth cocoon on the twig.

"Well, so much for reasoning with him," I said lightly. It was false lightness, but she needed it.

Suddenly she opened the jar and pulled out the twig. With her thumbnails she began picking at the cocoon.

"What are you doing, Rob? You're going to break it."

"I'm letting her out," she said. "That moth in there is trying to get out. See? She's beginning to break the cocoon here at the end, see? I'm going to help her get out."

She plucked away a chunk of cocoon, and the moth fell into her lap, its white wings limp and shapeless.

"She's tired," Robin said, dropping moth and twig gently back into the jar. "By morning she'll be flying all over the place."

I went to bed and lay listening to my radio and thinking my convoluted thoughts. Robin and Father and me, and Mother quiet at the edges of our struggle; Father's voice telling me as surely as God that I was unfit to survive without him; and the moth lying passive in Robin's lap.

The moth lived for two days and died without ever having mustered the strength to lift its wings.

18

Saturday night in the Hideaway Resort café. The place was full, mostly of men who had been fishing all day along the banks of the lake, where the ice was gone and the fish were waking for the spring. Rubber hip-waders and plaid shirts were the evening's dress code. The room smelled of sweat and rubber and fish scales, French fries and beer.

Scott and Doug were there with Jens and me. I was beginning to wonder seriously why they never bothered to get their own dates. They seemed content to hang around with Jens and me, and Jens seemed more than happy to have them. This was Phase Two of the courtship, I knew. Real life. We were past sweetheart rings and tender I-love-you's and into easy jokes, sometimes at my expense.

Jens' mother assumed I'd lend a hand behind the counter when the supper orders piled up, and I did it. I didn't mind swilling fries through the boiling fat or filling pitchers of beer from the keg. It wasn't my idea of an exciting Saturday-night date, but I went along with it, preferring to take a little pleasant fun where it presented itself rather than make an issue of going someplace nice, by ourselves. Jens was saving his money for college, just like Marlee, and I hated to have him spend unnecessarily on me.

When the supper rush was over I took a plate of onion rings and a Pepsi, and made room for myself at the table where Jens and company sprawled. They speared onion rings and munched.

"You're a real doll," Scott said, removing his boot from my chair so I could sit. "Old Jens doesn't know how lucky he is, having a broad like you to take care of him."

I snorted. "I hardly take care of him. Come on, you guys, those onion rings were supposed to be my supper."

"Oh, you take care of him all right," Scott said, grinning. He rolled his eyes at Doug, who punched his shoulder. Jens said, "Knock it off, you guys, you're embarrassing her."

They rocked their chairs back and laughed, and suddenly it dawned on me what they were talking about. They thought Jens and I were sleeping together. I boiled at the thought.

"Come on, Blondie." Jens pulled me up and onto the tiny cleared dance floor. The jukebox was blatting some old Beatles song. We danced, sometimes apart, sometimes bumping close together. Then, ignoring the beat of the music he locked me against him and started slow-dancing, breathing into my hair and humming a beat behind the music.

I stiffened away from him. This wasn't for me; this was for Scott and Doug. He was showing them his ownership of me.

We left at nine-thirty. Jens stuck religiously to Father's curfews. As soon as we were in the truck I lashed out.

"Jens, did you tell those guys that you and I were, you know, sleeping together?"

He lifted his hands briefly from the steering wheel in a gesture of innocence. "Would I talk about anything that personal with those jerks?"

"Those jerks are your best friends. Come on. You must have told them something. I could tell by those little remarks they were dropping, the way they looked at me."

"I never told them anything, honey. Honest."

"The subject of sex never came up between you and your two best buddies, in three months of taking me out? Come on."

He shook his head and smiled an oddly superior smile, as though he were playing mind games with a fool. "I never told them anything you wouldn't want me to."

But I knew he was lying.

19

On the first Saturday in April we had a late snowstorm. It started as rain in the middle of the afternoon, then sleet, then heavy fat snowflakes. By morning there were four inches and snow was still falling. As soon as I could bolt a bite of after-church dinner, I pulled the Gazelles out of their long nylon case and headed out.

There were no neatly packed tracks to ski in today. The warming-hut crew had put away the snowmobiles that pulled the track-laying sled. The going was slower and heavier than I was used to, with the Gazelles' slim red tips breaking their way through the snow's crust with every stride.

But the return of winter's breathtaking beauty was worth the extra effort. Mounds of snow humped the evergreen limbs, and an ice glaze made jewels of branches and weeds. By the time I was out of our woods and into the open meadow of the golf course, the sun had broken through, and its effect was dazzling.

Nothing mattered, not Robin's diminishment or the hovering threat of a future in the drug store or in Jens' café. A glory came up in me as I threw back my head, escaping my hood for the sun's touch on my hair. My legs were powerful. They pushed me off, stride to stride, forcing the Gazelles to cut and glide through the snow. My poles barely nicked the snow as my arms swung higher and faster.

Somebody up there had given me this perfect afternoon, and nothing that might come after it could tarnish the gift.

I went once around the intermediate trail, mushing down Wipeout Hill so slowly, in the unpacked snow, that I had to double-pole over the roller-coaster humps in order to keep going. Coming back toward the warming hut, I detoured onto one of the beginner-trail loops, where several people were skiing. A family group passed me, grinning and lifting poles in greeting, and I saw that Jason was skiing with their children. When he recognized me he snowplowed to a pretty tidy stop in front of me and made me watch while he pivoted one ski high in the air for an in-track about-turn. I'd started him on the maneuver, but he'd still been in the tipping-over stage at our last lesson.

I told him he was great, and skied on. I was getting sweaty and winded now. The warming hut looked good to me. I hadn't been sure the management would have it open today, since the season had officially closed two weeks earlier.

Marlee was there, sitting at the bar drinking a diet Coke and talking to Ben-or-Sam. She looked like a round rosy muffin in her tight brown pants and tan sweater.

"I went by your house and they said you were out skiing," she said. "I'll pop for a Coke. I just got paid."

We took our cups of Coke to the window bench and straddled it comfortably. The hut was temporarily empty except for us; everyone wanted to enjoy the skiing while they could, I supposed.

"So how's your love life?" Marlee asked when the small daily catching up was covered.

I shrugged and peered down into my Coke, staring at the ice cubes as though they held answers. "Same old thing. He keeps talking about wanting to get married right after graduation. I've told him what I want to do—you know, about going to Madison and getting a job. It's like he doesn't hear me. He can't seem to believe I don't want to marry him. I suppose he figures anything would be better than my present home life, that I should be jumping at the chance he's offering me."

"The chance to do what? Spend your life at Jensens' Hideaway selling fish bait? Even the drug store would be a step up from that, Air."

"Well, no, he keeps talking about getting into the University of Wisconsin this fall, with me working to support us till he gets his degree."

She snorted. "That's a lot of blue sky, don't you think? I mean, he's been out of high school a year now, his grades weren't especially good when he was in school, and come on, he wants to be a high school basketball coach when he couldn't even get on our varsity team. At a high school of three hundred kids. Where does he get off thinking he'd ever make it through college and into any kind of teaching and coaching job? I can see him just staying right where he is, making a nice lazy living at the Hideaway for the rest of his life."

I hunched my shoulders around my ears. What she said was too true to argue with.

"Another thing," Marlee went on in her reasonable, social-worker voice. "Have you ever asked yourself why this guy is so hot to get married at the tender age of—what is he, nineteen?"

A crooked smile pushed up one corner of my mouth. "Yeah. I figured he was counting on my paychecks to get him through college. Plenty of secretaries have put husbands through college before."

She drained her cup and crumpled it. "Well, that might be part of it. I hadn't thought about that. All I was wondering about was, well, now don't get me wrong. You're my best friend and I know you're a terrific person. You're skinny and pretty and kind and genuinely caring about other people. I know you would be a terrific catch for any man . . . but I'm not entirely sure Jens really knows that. I mean, I'm not saying this very well. . . ."

"He keeps telling me he loves me," I reminded her.

"I know that. But don't you sometimes get the feeling that he's sort of, well, clutching at you? That he's got giant insecurities of his own and he feels that you're going to save him some way? Now think about it, Arie. What nineteen-year-old guy is really mature enough to want marriage for any very solid reasons? They don't; not at that age. They're grabbing for something that has nothing to do with the individual girl involved. They're grabbing at, I don't know, manhood, or some sort of emotional security or whatever."

"Well? I'm grabbing too, you know. I need somebody to love me." My throat clogged and tightened.

"Of course you do," She smiled. "So do I. So does everybody. You've had a rotten deal from your father, I have a terrible weight problem, everybody's got something to fight. But I just can't see Jens Jensen ever being mature enough to give you what you need. Don't let the premature balding fool you." She grinned.

98

For a long time I looked out the window at the blue shadows stretching across the meadow from the bordering woods. The sky's bright blue was fading toward white now and graying again around the edges.

"You're probably right," I said at last. "I know I'm so desperate to get away from home that I'd do just about anything, and I know I don't really love Jens. Sometimes the things he says are so dumb they just set my teeth on edge." I shivered. "But at this point I honestly can't see any other way to get out from under my father."

She hit me across the leg. "Don't you dare marry Jens Jensen for any such stupid reason. I've told you I'd help you, and I will. How hard could it be?"

"It's the money," I said helplessly.

"Listen, I can get my mom's car. I can take you down to Madison right after graduation. I can lend you enough money to survive till you get a job. What are friends for?"

I shook my head. "I'll take you up on the ride, if things work out that way, but I'm not taking any money from you. It's going to cost a couple hundred, or close to it, even if I get a job right away, and even if I stay in the cheapest place I can find. Boarding houses with meals are around fifty a week, and most jobs pay twice a month, which would mean probably two or three weeks, minimum, before I got my first paycheck. You're still trying to scrape together your own bare minimums. And I'll tell you something else. The best way to kill a friendship is to start borrowing money, and you're the only friend I've got. I'm not taking chances with that."

As I left the warming hut a few minutes later, I paused to run my hands thoughtfully down the length of my apple-red glistening Gazelles. I stroked them with a lover's touch. They were freedom. My wings.

Yes. My wings.

99

20

As spring warmed toward summer, I often caught Father staring at me uneasily. He quit mentioning my work schedule at the drug store and talked instead about the family trip to Mackinac Island. I kept my secret plans locked in my head, and said as little to my father as possible, on any subject.

I worked on sewing projects, secretary clothes for the summer season. I studied the classified ads in the Madison Sunday paper and memorized phone numbers. I absorbed the rest of the paper, too, especially the ads and notices about new restaurants, the Madison Symphony, the Ski Club's spring party. Stubbornly, I willed myself into a new life.

Father decreed that my prom dress would be made for me by Mrs. Roys, who specialized in wedding gowns and formals. I would have been just as happy in something from Fashion Mart; the prom wasn't important to me. But he was fierce in his giving of this dress, as though he sensed it would be his last chance to soften me with gifts.

So I went for pattern choosing and draped fitting and basted fitting. The dress was a creamy froth. Such a waste, I thought, as I admired it in the mirror on prom night. Like a wedding dress—so much beauty and effort for so little time worn. This dress was for him, I knew, not for me. Sadly I stroked down its length and envied girls in lesser dresses whose fathers would be kissing them and sending them off to their proms in an aura of genuine paternal love and pride.

Tears ached up through my throat at the thought of all our years together, Father's and mine, all stained with our struggle, his to dominate me totally, mine to preserve my own essence in the face of his undermining.

And it would never get better, not as long as I lived in that house and gave him even token obedience, for his feelings toward Robin and Mother and me, whatever they were at root, were twisted by needs buried deep within him.

The prom was held every year at the Starlite Ballroom, a ramshackle barn of a place on the far shore of the lake. It was a leftover from the Big Band era, when weekend residents from Chicago held elaborate dances there. On the wall behind the bandstand were framed pictures of Benny Goodman, Glen Miller, and the Dorseys.

For our prom, there was only a small local rock band made up mostly of our own students. The music was so loud there was no way of telling whether they were good, but no one was in a mood to criticize.

The ballroom was a huge expanse of polished parquet floor, with stall-like booths in tiers around the edges. Father was there, shepherding Mother around by the elbow and acting the role of jovial chaperone. Most of the school-board members were chaperones; it was a high point of Heron

Lake's social season and no one wanted to miss it. But I felt he was there to watch me, to gather compliments about me from the other adults. "My, Ariel looks pretty tonight. You must be proud of her, Frank."

It was for this night that he had allowed me to cultivate Jens as a boyfriend, so that Father could stand among the other fathers and glow with possessive pride at the daughter he owned, all dressed up in his expensive gift, and looking like a happy graduate.

Who in this town would ever believe me or Robin if we tried to convince them that Frank Brecht was a destructive malevolence towering above our lives?

Jens looked almost handsome in his rented tux and lapel boutonniere. He had a wonderful time from the first dance to the last, pulling me onto the floor as often as I wanted, and filling in with nearby girls or the women chaperones when I ran out of steam.

It could have been a perfect prom if only . . . If only, I sighed. If only Father were absent or different; if only Jens were truly the love of my life; if only Marlee could have come. That last ache was closest to the surface. But no girl with any pride came to her senior prom without a date, and for Marlee no one had materialized. She had hoped, up until the last minute, that one of the less desirable boys would want to go to the prom badly enough to ask a fat girl. But no one had. She had talked about coming over earlier in the evening to watch me get dressed but had lost her courage and stayed away.

Life is going to make it up to Marlee for this night, I thought as I sat in our booth and watched Jens dance with my mother. Marlee is too good a person to go much longer without being appreciated and loved.

Late in the evening Jens led me out one of the side doors onto a rambling deck overlooking the lake. Several couples stood around the edge of the deck, at polite distances from one another, looking at the moon over the water and working out their private dramas.

Jens fished into his jacket pocket and brought up a tiny jewelers' box. I knew, sure as death, what was in it.

"Here's your graduation present, sweetheart," he said, and folded my fingers around the box.

"Jens, I can't . . ."

"Just look at it."

I opened the box. It was, of course, an engagement ring, a tiny chip of diamond almost lost in its gold setting.

"Oh, Jens, you shouldn't have bought that. You knew . . . we talked . . . I told you I didn't want to get married."

"Just try it on," he urged. I looked up at him, and any doubts I'd had melted away. He was pushing me to put on the ring; Father pushed me to accept the expensive dress. Jens ignored me when I told him what I wanted for my life; Father laid out work schedules for me in the drug store. Jens' methods might be softer, for now. He might merely be hoping the ring would tempt me into a commitment. But Father's and Jens' goals were the same.

I snapped the lid shut and jammed the box into his jacket pocket. "I hope you kept the receipt for that, so you can get your money back. I've told you and told you that I'm not ready to get married yet. You don't listen. I was wrong to tell you I loved you. It was what you wanted to hear and I was trying to please you, so I said it. But it's not true. I'm sorry, I don't want to hurt you, but you have to quit pushing, Jens."

He retreated, sulking. I put my arms around him and gave

103

him a squeeze, self-consciously aware that Father might be watching from inside.

"Listen, Jens, I still want us to go on seeing each other, I didn't mean that. I just don't think either one of us is ready for marriage yet. I've got a lot of junk in my head that I'll have to get sorted out before I can love any man. I've still got too much hate in me, from Father, you know? I'm going to have to live on my own a while and get that sorted out. And if you don't mind my saying so, you're not the most mature person I've ever known."

"What do you mean?" he pulled away, stung.

"I mean that I don't think you've learned how to love un-selfishly yet. But you probably will."

We eased toward each other then and stood side by side to look out over the lake. The lights of Jensens' Hideaway shone to our right, the brighter lights of town to our left.

When I had worked up sufficient courage I said, "Jens? I have a huge favor to ask."

"What?"

I pulled in a long breath. "I'm going to go to Madison right after graduation. I'm only going to have a tiny little bit of money to survive on, and I have no way of getting down there. Even bus fare would take too much. Marlee said she'd drive me down, but I don't want her to. If my father ever found out that she helped me, she'd lose her job, and she can't afford to do that. Will you drive me down there?"

I felt his body harden against my shoulder. "Like hell," he said.

"You won't do it?"

"No. Why should I? We talked about this before, Arie. I don't want you to go to Madison and work in some office full of guys in white shirts. How long do you think you'd be faithful to me, living down there? You've really got a nerve, you know it? Asking me to help you take off from me."

"Not from you, from Father." But I knew it was pointless to argue.

"I want you to stay here. So okay, you don't want to get married right away, but you could stay home and work in your dad's store like he wants, and save your money and then either this fall or next fall we could take off together, get married, get me into school somewhere . . ."

I stood away from him, shaking my head sadly. "You don't hear a thing I say, do you?"

I let him drive me home, for the sake of appearances, but we both knew it was over. I felt hard and dry inside, nothing more.

21

Most of the cars that left Heron Lake on Senior Skip Day morning went as scheduled to the Wisconsin Dells. One car, carrying just Marlee and me, lagged behind, got separated from the others in traffic in Stevens Point, and continued south, past the Dells turnoff, and into Madison.

Wedged sideways across the backseat of Marlee's mother's car was a long narrow nylon-cased bundle.

The road map had an insert showing Madison's major streets. The address we hunted was printed on my memory, one of several learned from Sunday paper ads.

The Ski Chalet was wearing its summer disguise, a patio store crammed with umbrella tables and freestanding hammocks. I shouldered my long bundle and sought the manager.

"We don't sell skis this time of year," the young man explained. "Come back around October, November. We'll have our next year's stock in by then."

106

"No," I explained again. "I don't want to buy skis. I want to sell mine. You can do that, can't you?"

He turned me over to another young man in the back room.

"I really need to sell my skis," I repeated. "I know it's not the season, but I need the money really badly. And they are good skis, almost new." My hands shook so that Marlee had to help me unzip the nylon carrying case and pull out the Gazelles.

"Well," the man said, and ran his hands over the spotless fiberglass finish, searching for nicks and scratches. "I couldn't give you full price for them," he said cautiously. "But they're in good shape, and it's a popular model. We sell a lot of Gazelles."

I held my breath, more than half hoping he would refuse. My escape plan would be impossible then, but at least I'd still have my beautiful, fleet, thoroughbred skis. But no freedom to use them, I reminded myself. Winter afternoons I'd be in the drug store looking out at the snow. No, this was the way. In a year or two I'd be able to buy another pair, with money grown from the seeds of these Gazelles.

He paid in cash, one-hundred-fifty dollars for skis, poles and carrying case.

Marlee treated us to lunch at a Burger King across from the Ski Chalet. The food rode like a lump in my stomach. Today was the turning point.

After lunch we consulted the street map again and drove past the three boarding houses whose ads and addresses I'd memorized. All were dingy places in depressing neighborhoods, but I looked at each as a potential launchpad for my new life.

The least depressing one was completely occupied. The

107

next one was for men only. I hadn't noticed that in their ad. The third one did have a vacancy, and the landlady showed us the room, but we backed away with polite murmurs of "I'll think about it." It had been filthy, with a large brown insect emerging from the sink drain as I peered in, and a smothering odor of mouse droppings in the air.

"So much for the cheap ones," I sighed as we climbed back into the car.

"I think you ought to wait till you get down here," Marlee said. "You could stay in the Y or somewhere for a few nights till you get a job. Otherwise you might end up living clear across town from work."

I shook my head. "Boarding houses are the cheapest. I've compared everything—rooming houses, the Y, every possibility. I thought I could get into one of these boarding houses and get a room and my meals for fifty a week. That way the skis money would cover two weeks of living plus a little for bus fares and lunches till the first paycheck. Now, I don't know."

We went into a corner café and pretended to be waiting for someone while I scanned the ads in that morning's paper. Only one sounded good, a women's boarding house at sixty dollars a week. I memorized the address and pulled Marlee away from the candy counter.

The house, when we finally found it, was a narrow white one sitting several steps above the sidewalk on a shady street on the near north side. The neighborhood was slightly better than the places where we'd looked earlier, and my hopes rose. I could live here.

The landlady answered my first ring. She was tiny and dark and wore a glaring orange sweat suit. When I asked about a room she shook her head.

"I'm sorry, honey. I just rented the last room a half hour ago. I won't have anything open for another week."

I brightened. "I won't want it till next Sunday night. Would you have one by then?"

She tipped her head and studied me with little beady bird eyes. "My Julie will be leaving this weekend, yes. She's been going to beauty school, don't you know, and her classes are finished then. I can show you her room. She's not home now, but she won't care if I show it to you. She's a sweet girl, don't you know. I'll be sorry to lose her."

Marlee and I followed the woman through a large sitting room all done in dark reds and blues. It was clean, though, and looked inviting. There was a piano in one corner, and several deep chairs with reading lamps. Marlee and I nodded to each other.

Up the open stairway and down a long hall; the little orange landlady opened a door and stood aside. We didn't go in, out of respect for the absent Julie, but we could see the whole room from the door.

It was small and had only one window, which looked out onto the house next door. Most of the room was filled by the bed, but there was an easy chair, a tall chest, a narrow closet and a low walnut table under the window.

Yes, I thought. It fell far short of the beautiful little apartment in my dreams, but that was for later. This was fine, to begin from.

I gave the landlady most of my skis money, for two weeks' rent and meals. She wrote out a receipt and entered my name and home address in a book in her diningroom. This Sunday night, I told her. That was my graduation day, and I'd be moving right after the ceremony.

If it kills me, I added silently.

22

We got lost trying to reconnect with the interstate going north out of town.

"If we stay on this street and keep going east," Marlee said grimly, "we have to run into it sometime."

We were on a boulevard in what must have been one of the wealthier areas of the city eighty years earlier. The trees down the center strip of the divided street were huge and graceful, and the houses were substantial. My architect-eye feasted on their towers and turrets and scallops. In one front lawn a couple was wrestling to erect a sign, and I thought what a shame it was to have the neighborhood scarred by even a tasteful commercial sign.

It wasn't until we were half a block past that the significance of the sign penetrated my wandering mind.

"Mar, turn here at this corner and go around the block."

"Are you crazy? We've already wasted more time than we should have. If we ever find this freeway we're going to have to shag to get home by the time the rest of the class is getting back from the Dells. You know yourself . . ."

"Don't argue. Turn. It probably won't amount to anything, but I have to see anyhow. There, where those two people are putting up that sign. Just pull in that driveway for a second. I'll be right back."

Without giving myself time to question my sanity or lose my nerve, I jumped out of the car and approached the couple. They looked like brother and sister, probably in their mid-thirties, both with curly brown hair and round, red faces. The red was from exertion. She was holding a wrought-iron signpost upright while he struggled to spill a batch of wet cement from a shallow mixing boat into the hole at the base of the signpost. Both of them wore denim cut-off shorts and T-shirts that advertised Nassau.

The woman was squinting at the signpost, trying to align it with the house across the road. An aluminum level lay in the grass, but it was beyond her reach and she couldn't let go of the post to get it.

I handed it to her. Startled, she looked at me. "Thanks."

I walked to the side of the post and squinted. "It's leaning just a hair to the north. No. Yes, there. That's perfect."

She shifted the post, checked it against the level, and smiled at me. "You have a good eye," she said.

On the ground near them, propped against its carton, lay the sign itself, with the lettering that had caught my attention from the car: Maitland and Maitland, Inc., Architects.

"Are you Maitland and Maitland?" I asked.

The man scraped the last of the cement mush out of the boat and turned a hose onto the yellow plastic, to rinse away the residue before it set. "At your service. I'm Maitland, and this is my wife, Maitland."

111

"I was just going past and I noticed you were putting up a sign that said architects, and I just thought I'd stop . . ."

Marlee came slowly across the grass, pulled by her curiosity.

"You looking for an architect, are you?" His eyes gleamed at the joke.

"No, but I'm looking for a job, and I just thought if you were opening a new office here, maybe you might be looking for a secretary or receptionist. File clerk. Anything at all."

He wiped his hands on his pants, bounced a quick look off his wife's eyes, and studied me. "What makes you think you'd want to work for us? Or are you just driving the streets looking for new offices opening up?"

I cleared my throat and got businesslike. "Actually we were trying to get back to the freeway and we got lost. My name is Ariel Brecht, and this is my friend Marlee Estes. We're graduating next week and I'm going to be moving down here to work, and we came down today to find me a place to live. I just stopped on an impulse when I saw your sign, because I love architecture and I may be studying it later, and if I could work for architects I could learn a lot."

"Let's hire her," the woman said. "Ariel is such a beautiful name, it'd be fun to have a secretary named Ariel."

"That's an intelligent reason," he shot back at her. I could tell they were well matched as a couple, and that good-natured sparring was the way they communicated.

To me he said, "Well, we were planning to look for someone in a week or so, when things got a little more sorted out here. I've been with a big firm downtown for several years, and Beth here has been working on her own, so now we're hanging out our shingle, as you can see. We can't afford a very high-priced secretary, at least this first year or so . . ."

"So let's hire her," Mrs. Maitland said again. "She's just out of high school, she'll be cheaper than an experienced secretary, and we can bring her up the way we want her."

I glowed a huge smile in her direction. Marlee eased away from us, now that she saw it was a business interview, and leaned against her car to wait.

He scowled thoughtfully at me, as though I were a piece of furniture he was thinking about buying. "Can you type?"

"Sixty-three words a minute with no mistakes. I've had three years of typing and office computers and business."

He grunted and motioned me into the house. "Our offices will be down here," he said, "and we live upstairs. It's pretty much of a mess."

The front room was spacious and elegant, with a bay window, a marble fireplace, and soft deep-green carpet. The walls were wainscotted in genuine cherry. I stroked the wood; I couldn't help it. Near the bay window was a small wooden desk piled with cartons of office supplies. A gray-green electric typewriter peeked out from the clutter.

The room behind this one, probably a dining room, now held a long table covered with blueprints. Off that were two smaller rooms, his and hers private offices where carpeting and wall-painting was still in progress. To the right of the workroom was a kitchen.

"This will be for coffee and lunches," he said. "And there's a little bathroom back there."

What a lovely place to work, I thought, with all my fingers invisibly crossed.

He led me back to the first room, to the little wooden desk with the typewriter.

"Okay," he said, "here's a piece of our new letterhead. Let me get the typewriter plugged in. There. Now, write a letter.

I'll just dictate to you while you type. Let's see, I'll make up a name. Mr. Joe Blow, of Joe Blow Incorporated, one-twenty-three Fourth Street, um, Wallbanger, Wisconsin. No, I won't dictate it; you just do it in your own words. Tell him his offer was crap and he should go to hell."

I looked up at him. He was watching me with steady eyes, weighing my reactions. I cleared my throat, hunched my shoulders to throw off their tension, and began to type.

"Dear Mr. Blow: Thank you for your letter of December first and for your offer. After careful consideration, my partner and I have concluded that your offer is unacceptable.

"Because of our full schedule of commitments at this time, I'm afraid we shall have to decline. Thank you again for your consideration. Sincerely, Maitland and Maitland."

It came out perfectly, not a single mistake, not even a strikeover. I glowed.

He read the letter, smiled at my translation, then sat on a corner of the desk. "Your hours would be nine to five, five days a week, an hour for lunch. We'd start you at five hundred a month and go up from there if you work out—and as our business picks up. Our budget is going to be tight at first, and of course since you have no experience . . ."

"That's fine with me," I said. My ears were ringing.

"When would you want to start? We really won't be ready for a week or so, but I suppose you could help with setting up the filing system and all that."

"I could start next Monday morning. I'll be moving down Sunday evening."

There was a heavy pause while we both weighed the import of the moment. Then he shook my hand and I was in.

He wrote down my name and the address of the boarding house and told me to apply for a Social Security card. "Well,

Beth will be happy," he said, standing and stretching. "She was afraid she was going to get stuck with the office work. She's actually a better architect than I am, but don't tell her I . . . oh Lord."

He ran out of the house. I followed more slowly; it's hard to move fast in a dream.

"Thanks a lot, buster," Beth yelled at him from across the lawn. "You go tooting off and leave me holding this damn post in wet cement. I didn't dare move for fear of getting it off center. Well, have we hired her?"

"Yes. Sorry. Here, we'll stake it in place till the cement sets."

She winked at me. "I hope you'll be able to stand us. I can't imagine any sane person wanting to work for this man, but at least I'm a wonderful person, so you'll have one human boss anyhow. Have you found a place to live?"

I waved vaguely. "A boarding house over on Capital—just till I start getting paid and can find something better."

Relieved of her post, she stepped away, flapping her hands to shake away their tension. "Oh, that's not too far. There's a bus. Actually you can probably find a nice little apartment right around here if you keep your eyes open. Lots of these big old houses have garage apartments, former servants' quarters, that kind of thing. Lots more personality than apartment-building cubes, and usually cheaper."

My smile widened. Marlee grabbed me in a heartfelt hug and, chattering, we drove away. It's all falling into place, I thought. All I have to do now is hold out through the last of the finals, through the graduation ceremony, and, somehow, through the getaway itself.

115

23

Between the high school and the lake shore was a long slop-
ing park and an old band shell where, on Sunday nights in
summer, there were under-the-stars band concerts. That day
the band shell held eighty-six gowned graduates.

I sat near the back of the sea of maroon robes, sweating
inside mine. My mortarboard pressed down against my forehead, its tassel catching my eye whenever my head moved.

The commencement address went on and on, but I was
glad. All my life I'd been pushing toward this moment, and
now things were spinning out of control.

Two rows in front of me and to the left, Marlee sat looking
surprisingly dignified in her gown, like an opera singer for
whom plumpness meant grandeur. She turned and gave me
a look.

The audience was seated in rows of gray folding chairs on
the slope of the lawn. Father and Mother were in the front

116

row, staring at me as if no one else existed. Robin was not with them. She was at home with the flu.

One of Robin's talents was the ability to make herself sick when it was convenient. She was home on this Sunday graduation afternoon with her manufactured flu and her assignment: pack everything I owned into whatever bundles she could make and get it all down to the side door.

As soon as the ceremony was over, Marlee was to slip away while I detained my parents, drive to my house and, with Robin's help, load the bundles, then come back. I would slip away when I had the chance, and we would be on the road for Madison before we were missed. Robin had the letter I'd written the night before, to Father and Mother.

But I didn't like it. I hated having Marlee involved, because it would certainly mean the loss of her job, which might in turn mean she wouldn't be able to find another summer job in time to make her fall tuition payment.

Knowing that her dream was as important to her as mine was to me, I'd argued all week against her insistence on helping. But I'd argued weakly; there was no other way I could get to Madison. Hitchhiking was the only alternative, and it was just too dangerous. Besides, Father would call in the highway patrol the way he'd done with Robin. Hitchhiking, I had no real chance and no way of carrying the clothes I'd need for my new life, all those things I'd made during the winter.

And I hated the sneaking. Planning the getaway had been exciting; doing it was just cheap. I didn't want Ariel Brecht to be this kind of person. What I wanted, I realized now, was a confrontation with Father. Honesty. But that was impossible without hanging Marlee.

Archie Wales, the mayor of Heron Lake and operator of

117

the Antlers, droned on with his commencement address. He gave the same address every year. I recrossed my legs. My eyes, wandering, met Father's and locked there.

As we looked at each other, odd messages tingled through my brain. He was afraid. He was afraid of me. Why? His expression was that of a man whose cruelly beaten dog is about to break its chain. Did he know what I was planning? Had he sensed the escape plan in my breathing and my movements this past week?

Was he afraid of losing me? Could it be as simple as that? But that would mean there was love in him somewhere for Robin and me. I didn't know. I was confused. His actions toward us from the beginning of our lives had been antagonistic. He was the power; we were powerless against him. Now that was shifting. I looked like an adult that day, sitting in my maroon gown and mortarboard cap.

He was losing me; we both knew it, and it was the knowledge of my elevation to a plane beyond his power that tingled in the gaze between us.

Our eyes held, and suddenly I felt strong. All my life I had fought this man, silently or openly, and now I knew that I had beaten him. No word passed between us, but in his eyes and in mine, all was said. We had fought and I had won. And his gift to me was the strength that our battle had built.

Without quite knowing where the wisdom came from, I understood then that although my friends might give me support, only my adversaries would give me strength.

Robin's moth appeared with startling clarity in my mind, and I knew that, by helping the moth out of its cocoon, she had robbed it of the struggle that would have strengthened its wings and allowed it to survive.

I smiled at Father, surprising both of us, for there was gratitude in my eyes. I saw him reach for Mother's hand.

We drove out of town singing, Marlee and Robin and I crowded into the front seat of Marlee's mother's car. The back seat was jammed with my bundles.

"I'm leaving," I had said to him, and he'd answered, "Yes." There was more said later, questions about where I was going and what my job was, but aside from some residual bluster there was no power left in him. The inevitability of my leaving seemed to stand alone, a thing created between us. Mother fluttered, Robin and Marlee stood back; Father and I faced each other, our eyes level and hard.

"And if you fire Marlee for helping me . . ." I said, having no threat to make but needing to make one anyway.

He glanced at Marlee.

Mother said, "He wouldn't do that, would you, Frank? You couldn't get along without Marlee, and besides, what would people think? There's nothing wrong with Ariel deciding to move to Madison. That's what youngsters do in a town like this, Frank. They get out of high school and move on to college or to a bigger town to get jobs. People won't think any less of our family if you let her go without making an issue of it. If you fired Marlee . . ."

I stared at Mother. The power of the weak, I thought. How many times in the past has she maneuvered him into doing what she wanted by allowing him to seem to dominate her?

She looked at me and her eyes filled; she loved me.

We loaded the car, and when Robin announced that she wanted to ride along, no one reminded her that she was sick.

119

It was going to be easier when Robin's time came, I felt instinctively.

I hugged Mother long and hard and promised to write every week.

Then I hugged Father, for the first time in my memory; I hugged him and I meant it. He was an imperfect man, a terrible father, but by surviving him I was more than I might have been without him. I was stronger. I was free!